BERN,
SON OF
MIKULA

BERN, SON OF MIKULA

MARIE HALUN BLOCH

Illustrated by Edward Kozak

Atheneum

1972   New York

*For my sister,
namesake of Olha*

A Note to the Reader

Readers usually want to know whether the characters in a story are real people. In this story about the Ukraine in the middle ages, Bern, the Princess Olha, her lady-in-waiting Malusha, and the commander Pretich were real people, for they appear in history. All the rest are imagined.

In writing the story of these people, the ancestors of modern Ukrainians, who lived more than a thousand years ago, I tried at the same time to picture as accurately as I could how people lived and how they thought in those faraway times and that faraway place. How they lived is best learned from the things they left behind that archeologists have found buried under modern Kiev—the pots and pans, the tools and weapons and furniture, the toys and ornaments, the foundations of city fortifications, of houses and other buildings. How they thought can be found out from what they wrote and from their traditions and customs that have come down to the present day.

But the story's the main thing—and I hope you enjoy it!

Guide to Pronunciation

Bern: "e" as in "end"
Elek: "e" as in "end"
Dnipro: Dni-PRO
Kiyan: Ki-YAN ("i" as in "in"; "a" as in "cart")
Pechenih: Pe-chen-IH ("e" as in "end")
Sviatoslau: Svia (one syllable)-to-SLOW

BERN,
SON OF
MIKULA

 He was awakened in the usual way by the foot prodding him as he lay on the hard clay floor and the hoarse voice of Long Face crying, "Up, boy, up!"

Bern sat up. Groggily, his head wobbling a little, he stared at nothing for a moment. Though the door of the hut was closed, he could hear the agonized groaning of the awakening river.

He shook his head to get the sleep out of his eyes. To his surprise, Long Face was putting on his sheepskin. Glancing at Bern, he said, "Come along! Don't go thinking about breakfast—there's no time."

He strode to the door and out.

Bern got shakily to his feet, picked up his cap, and put it on. That cap he would never leave behind, for it and its like had seen him through the thick and the thin of his short life. He picked up his sheepskin, which had served him for coverlet during the night, and stumbled after Long Face as he was putting it on. Last night's nightmare still clung to him. And here on top of that he was being deprived of breakfast. There were two parts of the day that held contentment and one of them was breakfast. (The other was when at last he lay down for the night.)

Out of doors, the sun had not yet climbed over the dense forest that covered the opposite shore of the river Dnipro and stretched far away to the horizon. A piercing wind blew in from the river, but already it carried a hint of warmth with it.

Until a few days ago, deep winter silence had lain over the waterfront. Then came the day when, as he had heard Kiyans say, a fish broke the thick ice on the river with its tail. Cracking into enormous blocks, imperceptibly the ice began moving southward, groaning ponderously along the way, to do battle with the approaching spring. The little harbor quarter was already starting to simmer with activity as Kiyans were beginning preparations for the summer's trading expeditions far away southward, across the sea to distant Tsarhorod.

The door of Long Face's hut faced away from the river, toward the high bluff on which the fortress-city of Kiev stood. When Bern stepped out of doors, as usual, he first looked up at the city surrounded by its massive earthen wall, above which jutted only a few roofs and that curious cluster of domes that he had noted on his very first day in Kiev. Those domes were always the first thing he looked for, and time and again he wondered just what they were. They were of different sizes and heights, and from them soared glittering golden crosses.

But it was not Bern's habit to ask questions. He tried to content himself with only distant glimpses of the city and what was in it.

Though by now he had been in Kiev for fully half a year, never once had he been inside its walls. For that matter, never once had he been in any city. To his former masters, the nomad Pechenihs out of Asia, a city was for plundering. And though they sometimes raided cities, they had never taken Bern along. Now that Bern lived in the very shadow of one, he often wondered what it was like, often wished he could see for himself, just once.

To the right of the city, on a high hill of its own, was a place surrounded by a palisade above which peeped a number of roof tops and towers. A banner fluttered from the peak of the tallest tower, whose roof glinted like gold.

But the cluster of domes topped with golden crosses at last lured his glance back to it. Several times he had tried to count the number of the domes, but from such a distance that was hard to do, for some were partly hidden by others.

Now Long Face, already at the gate in front of the hut, turned and said, "Come on!"

Obediently Bern hastened after him, out into the lane. Long Face's hut was one of the small jumble of log huts that sat higgledy-piggledy about the little harbor. In these huts lived and worked the handful of rope makers, sail makers, ship chandlers, and others who supplied the merchant-warriors of Kiev. Here and there were rather larger structures, in which the merchants stored the goods they had got together to trade with the Greeks at Tsarhorod.

When Bern had first arrived, more than six months before, the harbor quarter had resounded with activity from light to dusk, as ship after ship came home from the summer's trading and marauding, and the goods were unloaded and stored in the warehouses or carted up Borich's Wagon Road to the city on the height.

But as with each shortening day the sun had withheld more and more of its light, the activity had gradually slowed to a halt. Not long after the last of the ships had come sailing home, the first snow of winter had fallen. The harbor stilled and soon was locked fast in ice.

All through that long winter Bern had sat in Long Face's hut and helped make rope for next summer's boats. If he had ever thought of rope before that winter, he would never have imagined that there was so much to the making of it. First the bast had to be hackled—that is, split into fibres and combed. That was his task.

Then these short fibres had to be spun—twisted end to end into a long yarn. That task belonged to Long Face, for it took both skill and strength. It fell to Bern, however, to turn the spinning wheel. And even this simple, monotonous task took a certain skill, for if he did not turn the wheel at an even speed the thickness of the spun yarn would vary. Then Long Face would fill the air with angry shouts and later, sometimes, give him a cuff or two on the ear for good measure. Not until the yarns were spun could they be twisted into rope and the rope into hawsers.

Though Bern's hands had already been hardened from his former life, at first as he had bent over the hackleboard he had often scratched and cut them on the sharp nails studding it. Then, like as not, the cuts had festered. Sometimes the pain had been so insistent that he had had to allow himself a whimper. Gradually, however, his hands had healed and hardened sufficiently so that at last he could work the bast all the day long without suffering hurt.

6

For all that, he would not have said that Long Face was a cruel master. Indifferent, perhaps, but not cruel. For, during the livelong days he, too, worked hard. But Long Face had his cronies, who of an evening often came and drank mead with him, sang with him and called him brother.

Brother. Bern's thoughts always lingered over that word, not yearningly—only a fool yearns for a white raven—but wonderingly. What was it like to be called brother?

Abruptly, Bern was brought back to the present when Long Face, reaching the end of the lane, turned his back on the harbor and instead, to Bern's surprise, started up Borich's Wagon Road. He strode along so rapidly that Bern had almost to trot to keep up with him.

The turn had been so sudden that Bern's thoughts were set awhirl. Could they be going to the city at last? He looked up at Long Face, but found no answer there. Reluctantly, then, he pushed the exciting notion out of his thoughts. Better not to expect and not to ask, for that way disappointment often lay.

Though the hour was still early, a number of people were going toward the city or coming down to the river front. Bern kept his head somewhat lowered, but from under his straight dark brows he took note of the people all the same. First of all, with a certain satisfaction he noted that his cap caught a number of curious glances. And well it might, for it was a Pechenih cap, made of felt, rising to a hump on the crown, and with a flap along the back and sides to protect ears and neck.

As for the people themselves, Bern was struck again

by their general stature. The Pechenihs were a short, one might almost say a stunted, people. But Kiyans were tall and walked with long strides. Most of them had light brown hair like himself but some, like Long Face, were outright blond, with ruddy complexions. All were bundled in sheepskins against the cold. Under their sheepskins the women wore long gowns—that much was plain. Some—probably the matrons among them—wore headdresses that covered their hair, with two or three large rings dangling at either temple.

The men were clean shaven and wore their hair short, combed straight downward from the crown so that it looked like the thatch on a hut. Some, like Long Face, wore a single small earring for ornament.

Now and then Long Face glanced over his shoulder as if to make certain that Bern was still following. He could indeed have slipped away among the people and disappeared. But this possibility did not tempt him. On the contrary, among all those faces, the face and figure of Long Face was his sole security. For the others were total strangers, from whom one was foolish ever to expect good, whereas he had known Long Face for at least six months, and for good or ill, of all that world of people he was bound to him alone.

Once, as he hurried along beside him, Bern glanced back. In that glance he saw the great broken blocks of ice that choked the river. If the ice were solid he might have made his escape across it, to the forest on the opposite shore and beyond. Or, if the river were clear of ice, he might have swum across to freedom. But as it was, to venture on it now would end in his falling through the ice and being crushed or drowned.

8

But these were idle "ifs," every one. The truth was he lacked the courage to run away into the unknown.

Then there was the swampy forest of pine and scrubby birch growing all along the edge of the road, not ten leaps away to the right. Though the trees were thinly spread, so that one could see some distance into the forest, it stretched so far that one could not see all the way through it.

Nor did Bern have the courage to plunge into that forest and let it swallow him. For, for all his true origin, during most of his life Bern had known only the broad open steppeland far to the south, upon whose immensity one could see most of one's enemies from long, long distances. Even the steppe grass, though almost as tall as a man by midsummer, betrayed one's enemy, for by its movement one could tell whether it was being caressed by the wind or agitated by someone or something hiding at its roots.

But the forest—that was the abode of mystery, the lurking place of danger, the lair of strange and secret powers, mostly good, to be sure, but some evil. So he had heard Long Face and his cronies talk. Even among Kiyans, who lived their lives hard by the brooding forests, only timberers, huntsmen, and old women in search of herbs ventured into it. Ordinary folk stayed out unless they had urgent business therein.

A short distance into the forest, near the water's edge, stood a place called a church, St. Iliia by name. And some distance beyond that, still deeper in the forest, was the place sacred to the god Volos, patron of cattle and riches. Bern had heard Long Face discuss both of these at some length with his friends. The church, frequented by people who called themselves Christians—merchants, for the most part—was rather new. But the place sacred to Volos was no one knew how ancient. Plain folk, it seemed, stayed away from the church and that God that was worshipped there, for they had their own god-beings and their own belief.

By now they had reached the very foot of the bluff on which the city stood. And then came the disappointment that Bern had tried to guard against. Instead of continuing on up the road, Long Face suddenly turned to the right onto a broad path that was hemmed in on one side by the bluff and on the other by the swamp forest. The hope that had all the while been growing in Bern in spite of himself vanished. They could not be on their way to the city after all.

Disappointed, Bern tagged along at Long Face's heels. As they followed the path curving along the foot of the bluff, the great earthen wall of the city now loomed almost directly above them. Bern made bold to stop for an instant and stare up at it. Never had he seen a structure so commanding as that wall. As his glance reached the battlement along the top of it, he had the sensation of falling over backward. Just in time he looked away.

Still skirting the foot of the bluff, the path now led them sharply leftward. In another few moments, to Bern's surprise, it led them straight into a vale between the bluff on which the city lay and the hill on which the golden-roofed tower stood within the palisade. And down along the bottom of the vale curved a lane that was lined on either side with high fences, built of uneven wattles, behind which could be seen the ridges of sod roofs.

10

"Well," remarked Long Face. "Here we are—the potters' quarter."

Bern followed him up the lane until, near the middle of it, they came to a round structure about waist high. A gaunt frame stood over it, and to the side of the frame was fastened a large wooden wheel wound round with rope. A wooden bucket hung from the middle of the frame.

While Bern was staring at it, Long Face stepped up to it, seized the handle on the wheel and began turning it. The bucket let itself down by the rope and disappeared into the depths of the round structure, which turned out to be roofless and hollow. In a moment, a splashing sound came up from within the structure. Long Face let go the handle and motioned to Bern to take it and turn the wheel in the opposite direction.

The whole upper structure screeched protest as Bern turned the wheel. Presently the bucket came into view again—and it was brimming with water!

Long Face tipped the bucket, poured some of the water into his cupped hand and drank. Then, motioning to Bern to cup his hands, he tipped some of the water into them. Bern drank gratefully.

That well was the first that Bern had ever clapped eyes on. Down along the river front, people got their water straight from the river. And far away to the south, on the steppe, where the nomad Pechenihs roamed, they never troubled to dig wells, but drank from streams and springs and the Dnipro itself.

Bern looked into the black depth of the well, allowing it to draw him down, down, down into itself. Somewhere down there, far in the earth, water was talking. He awoke to something plucking at his arm. With an effort he brought himself up out of that well. "Come along," Long Face was saying.

Bern let his eyes travel over the marvelous machine of the well frame and windlass. Then, for the first time in many a moon his thin lips widened in a smile, not at Long Face, but at the world. What is sweeter than clear, cold water?

Long Face now led the way to a gate just opposite the well, pushed through it and strode into the yard. In the center of it stood a pair of huts, one built against the other. Though they were apparently of log, the logs were covered with white clay. He stepped up to the door of the larger one, on the left, and knocked.

In a moment it was opened by a boy with yellow hair that came down over his forehead and ears like a skull cap. His mouth was long and the lips thin, and there was a kind of contented, self-satisfied look to them, especially at the corners, which were turned upward and imbedded deep in the round cheeks. He wore the usual tunic and trousers, and he was barefoot. Bern knew at a glance that the boy, though somewhat taller than he, was about his own age.

Seeing Long Face, the boy's small blue eyes opened wide with surprise. "Uncle!" he cried.

 At the table within the warm hut sat a man and woman, neither young nor old. They both rose as Long Face entered with Bern in tow.

Atop the man's long, rather narrow face straight yellow hair grew to form a cap, like the boy's. Though his clean shaven chin was strong and firm, it was marred by a long scar of a cut that had healed badly, running from the left cheek, down and across the chin to the right jaw. So that, whereas the gleam in the blue eyes invited one to a possible friendliness, the ruined chin warned against.

The man's tunic, and his trousers as well, Bern had already noticed, were stained with splotches of various colors.

"Welcome, brother," he said as he rose. "How is it you're abroad so early?"

"Why, I have a little matter to attend to," Long Face replied.

"Sit down, do!" the woman said. The little ring of keys that she wore at her belt jingled faintly as she moved. She looked at Bern, her glance lingering for an instant on his cap. "And who is this?" she asked.

For all his months in Kiev, this was the first

Kievan woman Bern had seen near at hand. Before he could even note her appearance, he was struck by her manner, which seemed to say that she deemed herself quite the equal of the men present and had never even heard the word submissiveness. How different from the meek and self-effacing Pechenih women! Bern's hazel eyes darted from one to the other of the men. To his astonishment, neither made a single move to rebuke the woman.

Long Face sat down at the table. "Why, he's what I've come about," he said.

The man looked at Bern appraisingly. "Oho! Could this be the lad you captured from the Pechenihs last summer?"

"Pechenih!" the woman cried. "You've brought a Pechenih into the house?" Her voice rose. "But what are you thinking of, brother-in-law?"

"Calm yourself, sister-in-law," Long Face said. "He's not a Pechenih, but one of our own."

At this the woman subsided. Bern stole a look at her. Though he had been reading faces almost all his life just in order to survive, he had never seen one quite like hers—except that of the boy just now. For the face spoke the thoughts within as plain as noonday, and nothing was hidden in the eyes. They were as bold and outspoken as her words. It struck Bern that here was a person who would never do less than the decent thing—even if she did no more. Before her frank look Bern had to shift his gaze to the floor.

"What do they call you, boy?" she asked.

Bern uttered his name without looking up. "I am Bern, son of Mikula," he murmured.

"Bern—Bern," the woman repeated. "Bern, son of

14

Mikula." A frown appeared between her blue eyes as she tried to recall something. But then she shook her head. "And your mother?" she asked.

"He doesn't know," Long Face put in. "He was captured by the Pechenihs when he was a child and does not seem to remember his parents."

The woman paid no attention. "But who was your mother?" she persisted.

Bern kept his eyes carefully directed toward the floor. "I don't know who my mother was," he whispered.

This time it was the man who spoke. "Listen to the boy, will you? He speaks our tongue like a Kiyan."

"But of course, brother!" Long Face exclaimed. "Though—unfortunately for him—he grew up among the Pechenihs, he's one of our own."

"But does he know the Pechenih tongue, too?" Here the boy spoke up.

"Of course, Elek!"

"One of ours, you say?" the woman interrupted in her forward manner. She was looking him up and down. "Well, yes," she said at last. "His image is like, for all the mouse hair. That much I'll grant you. But why does he cringe and cower so? Like a whipped dog."

Long Face laughed. "But that's only the Pechenih manner, sister-in-law! You've never seen one, else you'd know. It's their notion of politeness."

"It is? Truly? You mean to say they all cower before each other?"

Long Face laughed again. "Why, no! But this one, don't forget, was their captive."

There was a silence while all considered this. Now

for the first time Bern noticed that on the stove in a corner of the room sat a pot and from it vapor was beginning to rise. Hungrily he watched it.

The woman was the first to speak. "I don't understand it. I don't understand it at all!" Suddenly she turned on Bern. "Look up!" she commanded.

In distress Bern glanced at Long Face.

"Be still, wife, I tell you," the man said. "Let us hear what our brother has to say."

Once more the woman quieted.

"I think to go on another voyage, come June," Long Face began. "What's to keep me home? Wife dead, daughter married off—and it's a jolly life, hard though it is."

The man nodded agreement, but the woman only stared steadily and unsmiling at Long Face.

"So," he went on, evidently unperturbed, "I've brought you the boy. He's all of a dozen years old and in another year you'll have yourself a man in him. In the meantime, he'll be of great use to you—works from sunup to sundown without complaint. Learns fast. Already he knows almost as much about rope making as I do. No doubt he will learn the mystery of tile making as quickly."

"If he is so skilled at rope making, brother-in-law," the woman interrupted, "you keep him."

"Impossible!" Long Face protested. "I mean to sail with the first ship that goes this summer."

"But that's not for two months yet!" the woman cried.

"I know," Long Face replied, his voice edgy with impatience, "but meanwhile I must help with the preparations. There's always a great deal to do before

16

going on a voyage."

"Then make him help you!"

"But I won't have time to keep an eye on him either now or during the voyage—especially down there where we have to drag the boats past the cataracts and at one and the same time keep a sharp lookout for the Pechenihs. He might run away."

"Then let him. Let him go back to them!"

The man had been silent all this while, but now he spoke. "Just a little moment, wife. He could be of use to us after all. As it is, lately, even with Elek's help, I have not been able to keep up with commissions for my tile. There's the Princess' new church, don't forget—in which she wishes not just part, but the entire floor paved with mosaic and tile, after the manner of the Greeks. Then there's the new palace of the merchant Borich that's abuilding, and that will need ornament—not to mention the new palace that the commander Pretich thinks to build himself."

He turned and looked Bern up and down. "He's skinny as a reed, true, and looks as though there's precious little strength in him, but tile making takes none to speak of. A child could do it, when it comes to strength. Yes, I'll take him off your hands, brother."

This was altogether too much for the woman. "And add another mouth to feed?" she cried shrilly.

"What of that, wife? Are we so very poor?"

"But just look at him, will you? A magpie found him on a rubbish heap. And skinny as a reed, just as you said. He'll eat for two!"

She paused for breath, but before she could go on, the man checked her.

"I tell you, wife, be still. Don't let me have to speak to you for the third time." The scar across his chin had deepened and darkened. "We'll keep the boy and that's an end. So just bring forth a pitcher of mead, wife, and we'll drink the drink to seal the bargain."

During all this hot exchange, Bern stood silent, his eyes, except for fleeting glances, fixed on the ground. Though he was the subject of their argument, they paid him no heed. Only the boy—Elek by name, evidently—gave him even so much as a glance. Bern saw all this not by looking directly at any of them— that he would never have done—but furtively from the corners of his eyes or from beneath his brows, shifting his eyes without moving his head, in the Pechenih manner.

At last, the bargain drinks drunk up, Long Face rose. He said his good-day to each, his thanks, and then turned to go. As he passed Bern on his way to the door, he threw him a look of triumph.

From the corner of his eye, Bern watched him go to the door and out. He suppressed a sigh. Long Face hadn't been a particularly good master. But good or not, at least he had been a familiar one and Bern had learned well enough what to expect at his hands.

But here, now, were new masters. Unfamiliar, the woman hostile—all over again he would have to learn a master's ways.

The woman now came and stood in front of Bern. She looked him over again, up and down. She was rather tall, more plump than not, and wore the usual long gown belted at the waist. Sandles on her feet.

From beneath her matron's cap strayed strands of brown hair. At either temple of her headdress hung a pair of copper rings. She wore no other ornament. She had a rather short nose and a mouth set with exactly the same complacence as her son's.

Now she walked all around Bern and at last came to a stop in front of him again. She stood, her arms folded across her bosom, and slowly shook her head, the corners of her mouth pushed back. Bern for his part stood carefully looking down at the floor, as he had many times seen captives do in the Pechenih camps.

"But what makes him quail so?" she said to her husband, her voice rising in exasperation. "Does he think that I mean to strike him?"

She reached out a hand, gingerly plucked up one of Bern's long, matted locks and said something to her husband. Bern stood stockstill, tense. If she seized his cap . . . But she did not touch it.

The man nodded and spoke to Elek. That one left the hut and in a moment returned holding a sharp, double-pointed weapon. He handed it to his mother.

The man then took a step toward Bern. But Bern was ready. He ducked out of reach, looked wildly around, and then streaked headlong for the open door and out. Halfway to the gate, as ill luck would have it, he tripped on nothing at all and fell flat.

In the next instant the man was upon him and pinning his shoulders to the ground. With all his might Bern twisted and turned and beat his legs. To no avail. The weight of the man's knee on his back only increased and Elek, it seemed, came and sat on his legs. But soundlessly Bern continued to struggle.

20

The man shouted something. His wife approached, the double-bladed weapon in her hand. She stepped around to the back of him and plucked off his cap, which till now had stayed on his head. Desperately Bern redoubled his contortions. He managed to twist one leg free, but the boy caught it again and held it fast.

In the next instant Bern felt cold iron at the back of his skull. Snip! He was so surprised that he paused in his struggle. Snip! He tried to turn his head to see what the woman was about. But the man seized the top of it with his big paw and held it fast. Snip! Snip!

Bern went limp. It was no use.

At last the woman stepped away. The man lifted his knee off his back and let go his head. Elek stood up. Bern lay still for a moment longer. Then slowly, cautiously lest they all leap on him again, he sat up. Strewn on the ground all around him were long locks of light brown hair. He put a hand to his head.

They had shorn him. As if he were a slave, they had cut off his locks.

And that was by no means the last of the ignominies he was put through that day. At a word from the woman, the man and boy seized him again, marched him straight to a trough filled with water that stood in front of the hut, stripped him of his sheepskin, of his ragged and dirty tunic and trousers, all crawling with lice, and plunged him into the cold water. Afterwards, the woman brought out another tunic and pair of trousers, patched but clean, and he was made to put them on. She took away the sheepskin and spread it on the ground in the sun.

The man now nudged him across the yard toward

21

the little hut next the dwelling, thrust him in, and shut the door. Bern could hear the hasp on the door being swung over the staple and the pin dropped in.

Shorn and shivering, Bern sank to the floor and leaned against the wall. Strips of golden daylight came through the chinks in the door. He sat dumb, hugging his knees, his thoughts muted.

Slowly he became aware of voices and looked up. Evidently this hut and the dwelling next to it shared a common wall, for from that direction the voices came clear.

"Very well, wife." That was the master's voice coming through the wall. "It will be as you say. If it turns out that he is not earning his keep, we'll give him back."

"But won't uncle be displeased?" Elek's voice.

"Why, let him be displeased," his mother spoke. "He gave the boy to us and we took him as a favor. As a favor, don't forget." She paused, then uttered a sound of disgust. "But if only he wouldn't cringe so!" she cried.

"Yes, yes," the master spoke again, irritably this time. "Let us not keep chewing the matter over like a cow her cud."

Bern put his head down on his knees. All that mattered was that he had lost his cap. He had to have it back. If need be, he would plead for it.

 Bern sat by the door, shivering and staring at the big conical shaped oven built into a corner of the hut. It was stone cold. If only the mistress would give him back his sheepskin! After all, it was still only early April.

At last the cold and his unappeased hunger would not let Bern sit still. He got to his feet and began moving about the room. Opposite the door, mottled golden light filtered through a small window covered with a skin. But when he went over to roll it up and look out, he found it fastened down with pegs.

Taking up most of the room was a long stout table, rough hewn of two slabs, its legs thrust into the hard-packed clay floor for greater steadiness. Along one side of it, nearest the door, was a long bench.

Besides a small iron brazier and a little basket of charcoal, a variety of little clay jars of different shapes and sizes stood about on the table. Bern carried several of them to the light of the window and peered inside. They contained powders of various colors— blue and green, brown and yellow. Bern recognized them as the source of the stains on the master's tunic. Some of the little pots had two compartments, with a different color in each. One pot, however, was somewhat larger and made of stone; a thick iron stick jutted out of it. Inside it were traces of the same colors.

On one end of the table lay a number of shallow wooden boxes, divided inside into small squares and oblongs of different sizes, each filled with clay. Bern poked a finger into the clay and found it moist and soft.

Turning away at last, he noticed a stack of tiles of different sizes and shapes in the corner near the window. He went over and stood looking at them. Finally, out of curiosity, he picked one up. It was square, about half the size of a man's palm. One side was a dull yellow brown in color, but the other was shiny and covered with a tracery of design in two colors.

As Bern looked over all these things he wondered just what their use was. He could understand the clay from which the tiles were formed, and even the wooden forms on the table in which the clay was shaped into tiles. He even understood that the oven in the corner, taller than himself, was the kiln in which the tiles were baked. For, even the Pechenih women made clay cooking pots of a sort and many a time Bern had had to gather fuel for the hot fire needed to bake them hard. But the uses of the brazier and the other things on the table were a mystery to him.

At last he went back to his place near the door, to the right of which stood a large wooden tub with a big wooden mallet in it. Idly wondering its use, he sat down and leaned his back against it. His hunger had grown. Yet, even if there had been someone to ask for food, he would not have done it.

He did not know how long he sat there, but at

last he heard footsteps approaching. Perhaps food was being brought. He scrambled to his feet. Someone was pulling the pin out of the hasp. In a moment the door swung open, creaking on its leather hinges.

Elek came bounding in, bringing with him a blaze of sunshine. He had a laugh on his face. On his head, flap to the fore, sat Bern's cap.

With an outraged cry, Bern made a lunge for it. Laughing, Elek ducked. As he did so, the cap fell off. Bern lunged again, and at the same moment Elek, still laughing, slapped his foot on it. Bern fell full length, grabbed Elek's ankle, and tried to remove it, tugging at the cap at the same time.

To no avail. He glanced up at Elek and that one, evidently seeing something stricken there in Bern's face, suddenly sobered. Staring at him, a puzzled look on his face, slowly he lifted his foot and backed off.

Bern snatched up the cap and with both arms held it close against his chest, looking up at Elek with defiant eyes.

With a shrug of his shoulders, Elek turned away. Going around the table to the window, from a heap of sacks that lay there he picked up several. Then he took up a pick leaning against the wall and hoisted it onto his shoulder. "Come along," he said to Bern, and led the way out of the hut.

Bern put the cap firmly on his head and obediently followed. Out of doors the master stood waiting, at his feet a large square board with a rope fastened to it. It was a little sledge. With a jerk of the head he indicated to Bern that he was to drag it along and follow. Bern picked up the rope, threw it over his shoulder, and trudged after the master and Elek as they made for the gate.

From the doorway of the dwelling, the mistress called after them. "Mind that he doesn't run off!" But there was a laugh in her voice, as if she already knew that there was no danger of that.

The master made no answer.

Out in the lane, instead of turning down the street —the way Bern had come with Long Face that morning—they turned in the opposite direction, toward the top of the lane. To their left, high on the bluff, loomed the city. But, though Bern searched eagerly for the familiar cluster of domes, from this side they were not visible.

As he trudged along after the master and Elek, staring up at the city, again he wondered what it was like within those walls. It could not be the same as the Pechenih camps. For, although those camps were large, with several thousand people crowded together, they could not properly be called cities, for they were composed only of tents that could be struck at a moment's notice whenever the chiefs had decided that the camp should move on.

Along the potters' lane were no more than half a dozen huts on either side. When they had passed the last of these, there in front of them was the bare slope of the bluff. Here and there, water was seeping out of the yellowish grey clay. All along it, at about the height of a man, large holes had been gouged.

"Give him the pick," the master said to Elek, "and let him dig while we fill the sacks."

By now Bern was fair dying of hunger. But there was nothing for it. He took the pick and began gouging out clay while Elek and his father held the mouth of one of the sacks open to catch the loosened chunks. The clay, still not entirely thawed, was hard as rock. Foothold was slippery and treacherous, for the water oozing out trickled down and muddied the ground. But by steady effort Bern managed to loosen big chunks of the clay. He had a chance to rest briefly when one sack was filled and, hauling it aside, they fetched an empty one in its place. But he was digging more and more feebly.

At last, to his relief, came respite. Two others, a man and a youth several years older than Elek, arrived dragging a sledge. They turned out to be neighbors to the master. While the two men stood talking, Bern took the chance to slacken his work. Behind him Elek and the youth talked and laughed like good friends. Evidently Elek was explaining Bern's presence to his friend, for among the indistinct words he caught his name being repeated. In a few moments the man and youth went on, farther along the bluff, and Bern had to begin digging in earnest again.

The sun had reached its day's zenith before they had the three sacks filled. They were so heavy that even the master was unable to lift them. Instead, they tied each with a rope and one by one worried them onto the sledge. It took the strength of the three of them to drag the sledge homeward.

On the hill ahead of them was the place surrounded by a palisade that Bern had so often wondered about. He could see now that the banner atop the golden-roofed tower was emblazoned with a device of some sort. That tower must be taller than three, and even four, huts set one atop another!

Gazing up at it, Bern marveled at its height and wondered how anyone could have built it. Though all the morning he had been afraid to utter a word of his own, now at last he could not help himself. "What is that?" he asked.

Elek turned to him with a mocking laugh in his eye. "Oho," he said, "it talks."

Bern dropped his gaze. He should have kept his mouth shut.

"That's Castle Hill," Elek went on. "And that stone tower you see is part of the castle belonging to our Princess. There's a castle within the walls of the city, too, and another, also of stone, just outside it. And this one, where now she prefers to stay."

Bern stared up at the castle again. Long, narrow green eyes, he now saw, glinted from it. He wanted to know what made the windows glint green. He wanted to know the name of the Princess. Especially he wanted to know who had built the castle. He wanted to know—all of a sudden, he was bursting with questions. He wanted to talk to Elek.

He wanted to talk!

But he didn't dare. He might only earn himself a cuff on the ear—or, even worse, a laugh.

When they reached home at last, they pulled the sledge right into the workshop and rolled the sacks off onto the floor under the window.

When they had done that, the master said to Bern, "Now you stay here."

Going out with Elek, he closed the door and fastened it shut. Bern felt too weak even to feel amusement at this. The furthest thought from his mind right now was escape. He was so weak that he could not have run a step.

He took off his cap and hid it carefully within the bosom of his tunic. Then, laying himself down on the floor near the wooden tub, he shut his eyes. A murmur of voices was coming through the wall, but he could not even make the effort to listen. Whether he lay there a long or a short time he could not have said. After a while he heard the door being unfastened. He sat up.

The door opened and Elek came down the steps again, this time carrying a steaming bowl. He held it out toward Bern. "Your dinner," he said.

With a swift movement Bern got to his knee and snatched it from him. There was the usual wooden spoon, but Bern had never learned to use one. The Pechenihs ate with their fingers. Pushing the spoon aside, he scooped up a handful of the hot porridge in the bowl and thrust it into his mouth, keeping his eyes on Elek as if he feared that he would take the bowl away from him.

Elek was staring at him in astonishment. "Hey," he said, "didn't my uncle give you breakfast?"

Bern only shook his head briefly.

"You poor wretch," Elek said, "you should have said something!"

Without pausing in the business of stuffing his mouth, Bern stared up at Elek, his eyes speaking as much resentment as he dared let them. Never ask for anything, for fear of refusal. Never put yourself forward, for fear of rebuff. Always wait for the first move from others. Those were the rules he had taught himself among the Pechenihs and those were the rules he lived by.

29

"My mother has a sharp tongue sometimes," Elek went on, "but she's really not a bad sort."

Now it was Bern's turn to be astonished. Not a bad sort? He stared up at Elek.

Elek glanced away. Then he said, "I don't think there's any more, or I'd ask to have your bowl filled again."

Bern made no answer. He was busy licking the bowl clean and then the spoon. Taking the bowl at last, Elek turned to go. But he paused and said, "I could bring you a piece of bread . . ."

For answer, Bern turned his back on him. After the episode of the cap, he could not be trusted.

But even while he was doing this, he was regretting it. He was regretting denying himself the bread, of course. But more than that, he was regretting rejecting Elek's mild offer of friendliness—if that's what it was. He could not remember when anyone had been as friendly as that to him.

As the door was closing, Bern sat hugging his knees in despair. He put his head down on them and gave a soft groan. Rarely did he strike out at anyone. But here he had struck out at the wrong one.

At dusk that day, Elek came in with Bern's sheepskin and dropped it beside him, saying, "Here. You'll probably be glad for this come night."

Bern gave him a quick ghost of a smile. But Elek was already going to the door and did not return it.

Early the next morning the master came into the kiln hut, Elek at his heels. "To work! To work!" he cried cheerfully. "You, son, show the boy the mysteries of preparing the clay. From now on you will be relieved of that task. You ought in any case to be perfecting your other skills in our craft."

Elek seemed pleased. "Come on," he said to Bern. "First we have to fill this tub with clay."

Leading the way to one of the new sacks of clay they had brought, he began breaking off large lumps of it while Bern carried them one by one over to the wooden tub near the door and dumped them in. Back and forth he trudged until the tub was half filled.

Then Elek came over and, handing the wooden mallet to Bern, said, "Now then, you must first break up these lumps of clay with this mallet. From time to time temper it with a little water from that jug over there. When you have got it soft enough to work, get into the tub and knead it with your feet. Keep tempering it. Last of all, knead it with your hands till it's as smooth and fine as dough. And all the while be sure to keep plucking out the stones and sticks and other matter that you will find in it. So there you have it. Understood?"

31

Bern nodded. Kneeling down in front of the tub, he began vigorously pounding the lumps of clay. What an easy task they had given him! The hard clay soon proved to be so unyielding, however, that in a little while his arms began to ache, and now and again he had to dare pause for a few moments. But, feeling the eyes of the master on his back, he quickly resumed the pounding.

It must have been nearly noon before Elek at last pronounced the clay soft enough to work with the feet. Gladly enough, Bern climbed into the tub and began capering about on the clay with his bare feet, while Elek stood watching. "No, no," that one said after a moment. "Just dancing about on it won't do. You've got to tread heavily—else you'll be at it till doomsday."

Chagrined, Bern obediently began to plod, moving his legs heavily up and down. Elek watched for a moment and then, satisfied, returned to his own task.

As Bern kept plodding up and down, up and down, the feel of the yielding clay squeezing up between his toes was pleasant. But after a while that, too, began to prove dull work, and tiring as well. He was glad when at long last the mistress came in to say that dinner was ready and the work came to a halt.

She brought with her a bowl of broth and a chunk of bread for Bern. He took them from her with that exaggerated show of gratitude that he had learned from the Pechenihs. She watched the performance for an astonished moment, then flung up her hands and left, followed by the master and Elek. In a moment Bern could hear them in the dwelling as they sat down to their own meal.

Bern thrust the chunk of bread into the bosom of his tunic to save till later. Then hungrily he lifted the bowl of broth and, though it was almost too hot to bear, drank it down to the last drop. At the bottom, to his complete surprise, he found two pieces of chicken, a wing and a neck. He set the bowl down and, with a feeling of luxury, plucked out the wing. After gnawing all the meat off the bones, one by one he cracked them in his teeth, noisily sucked out the bit of sweet marrow, letting the discarded pieces of bone drop to the floor. Never had he tasted anything so good! On the neck, when he finally got to that, he found a goodly piece of tasty fat.

He could hear them talking now next door. The master and Elek were discussing some newly formed tiles and their plans to set them out of doors to dry in the sun if weather permitted on the morrow. They did not speak of Bern or his part in the work at all. Gradually the talk quieted.

When, after noon rest, the master and Elek returned to the kiln hut, the mistress came, too. Bern stood up from his sheepskin, where he had been drowsing. The mistress, noticing the little pieces of broken chicken bone strewn all around him, frowned and pointed to them. "Is this how they do where you come from?" she cried sharply. "Pick them up and put them in the bowl!"

Bern hastened to do so. The mistress took the bowl and went out.

Bern resumed his task of plodding up and down on the clay. Whatever eagerness he'd had for the work had long since vanished. But at last, toward mid-afternoon, when Elek gave him the word, he climbed out of the tub.

He took to kneading the clay with his hands, picking out the stones and sticks as Elek had instructed him. After what seemed like a long while he thought surely he had kneaded that clay so smooth that it could not possibly be got any smoother.

Now the master came over, bent, and pinched off some of it. He stood rubbing it between his fingers, staring thoughtfully upward. "Aha," he said at last. "A little more and this batch will be ready."

Disheartened, Bern resumed his task. Several times more the master came over and tested the clay, each time only to pronounce the verdict, "A little more . . ."

At last, however—but not until nearly dusk—he said, "That will do for this batch."

Bern sat back on his heels and sank his chin to his chest.

When he was locked in for the night, some of the lingering daylight was still coming in through the window and the rather wide gap between the bottom of the door and the threshold. He spread his sheepskin, fleece side up, on the floor in the corner nearest the door but out of the way of the wind that now came whistling through the gap at the bottom of the door. He lay down on half the sheepskin and drew the other half over himself. But he did not close his eyes.

He did not mind the dark. Indeed, it had always, as long as he could remember, been his friend. For it meant that the long day of doing others' bidding was over. The respite would only last the night, but he cherished it.

Among the Pechenihs almost always, except in the

depth of winter, he slept out on the steppe, with the spangled sky for roof. Bern stared up into the darkness and thought about those nights. And hopeless yearning for the steppe came over him, for the grand sky and the sight of the plumed feather grass bending under the wind.

He was brought back to the kiln hut by the sharp reports of the ice on the river cracking as it moved toward the distant sea. Its snapping and groaning had become almost continuous, so that only now and again was he any longer aware of it. With a stirring of something curiously like homesickness, he thought of Long Face down in the harbor quarter. Not that his hut was any better than this. But at least it had become a familiar place.

That night, whether because of the tormenting lice that still infested the sheepskin or from some other reason, Bern slept only fitfully.

 Bern woke in a sweat. As in a dream, he listened to a shout hovering in the darkness of the hut. Again men's yelling rang in his ears as the Pechenihs went galloping headlong down upon the shore, where the merchants' men were struggling to drag their ships on timbers past the cataract.

Bern stared into the dark. He felt himself galloping with the band of Pechenihs yowling above the roar of the cataract and loosing clouds of arrows into the struggling men. Then, suddenly wheeling and retreating for a distance, the Pechenihs wheeled and charged again, over the killed and the wounded, straight for the ships left lying on the timbers.

Not a soul to raise hatchet or spear against them, the Pechenihs dismounted. With happy shouts they raced for the boats and swarmed over the sides, laughing over their easy victory.

But just as they fell to pillage, out from hiding places leaped the merchants' men, hatchets swinging. The Pechenihs rushed for the sides. But before they could scramble overboard, most of them were caught and cut down.

Some few, Bern among them, got over the sides

and made a dash for their horses. But their short legs were no match for the long legs of the merchants' men. They were easily overtaken and hacked down, almost to a man.

As for Bern, he stumbled and fell, wrenching his ankle so badly that when he tried to get up he only fell down again. While he was still on his hands and knees struggling to get to his feet, the merchants' men were already straggling back after their short work. A pair of them halted in front of Bern.

Bern looked up. Over him stood a man, hatchet raised. But his companion, a man with a long face, shouted something and that one lowered his arm without delivering the blow. Then the two men seized him under the arms and lifted him to his feet.

Now Bern tried to fight loose. He fought like a dragon. But they were too much for him, of course. All the same, he had fought . . . That fact, whenever he came to it, always gave him a rare satisfaction.

It was not till much later that Bern knew that the reason he had been spared was that the men saw that he was not a Pechenih at all, but of the Slavic race, as were they themselves. That was not difficult to tell, of course, for the Pechenih was out of Asia and looked it.

When Bern came to, it was to the sound of water quietly slap-slapping against wood. He listened for the cataract but could not hear it. Boards creaked and rocked and resiliently contorted beneath him. He opened his eyes. He was in a boat, and the same long face was leaning over him. The face was saying something, in a tongue long unfamiliar to Bern. He closed his eyes again and with an effort of memory knew that the face had said, "He's coming to."

Bern frowned. His first raid and this is how it had ended. Though he had been among the Pechenihs for nearly eight years, always before this they had kept him and the other captives shut up in a tent during a raid, and under watch. But that day for the first time he had been ordered to go with the men. There, now, was a thought to savor . . .

Now here he was a captive again, just as once before he and his mother together had been captives of the Pechenihs. As always on the rare occasions when he recalled his mother, his thoughts came to a pause. He saw her anxious, troubled eyes. "Above all, remember your name, my little son," she would say. "Bern, son of Mikula. Now repeat after me . . ."

For some reason, he did not remember his mother's disappearance soon after their capture. He had been put among the Pechenih boys, ate with them, slept all of a heap with them, played with them . . . And all of a sudden one day, as he ran with them across the immensity of the grassy steppe after some horses, it came to him: his mother was no longer there in the camp. She was gone. He must have been a year older by then.

From then on, as year flew after year, he learned the Pechenih tongue, learned their ways, learned to ride the tarpan, the swift wild pony of the steppe, learned to shoot with bow and arrow, learned other manly skills.

To all appearances, Bern became a Pechenih. Except that—he frowned into the dark of the hut over the searing thought that came to him now—there was that final, invisible, and insurmountable barrier between him and them. Though nightly he had sat with the group around the campfire, his appointed place was never anywhere but on the edge of it. This much he had to admit to himself.

From the talk around those campfires Bern learned that the true home of the Pechenih was far to the east. But their ceaseless search for good pasture for their flocks of sheep and herds of cattle had led them westward, ever westward, until at last they had reached the Dnipro River. There, astraddle the river just north of its delta, they had taken up their abode. Around their campfires they often talked longingly of their ancestral home far away within the depths of Asia. But not a word was ever spoken of returning there. They preferred to occupy others' land, lush with grass and teeming with herds of the wild tarpan.

Bern never thought of escape. At first, he had been too small for such thoughts. And then—where would he have run to?

Only now and again did he have a passing thought of his own people, those that he had sprung from, and that only after a raid, when the Pechenihs usually seized new captives. Some of these sickened of home-longing and soon died. Some were sickened by the ropes around their necks by which they were led and seemed to die of that. Others died more sensibly of wounds or ailments.

Usually, however, a goodly enough number managed to survive. Then, hearing their talk, something would stir in Bern, but by that time it was nameless and unnamed, it died. He had all but forgotten his native tongue. But the music of it—that he did not forget, and he never failed to know it again whenever he chanced to hear it among the captives. Yet among themselves even they at last spoke only a mixture of their own and the Pechenih tongues. Sometimes, evidently seeing something of home in Bern's features, they tried to talk to him. But he always narrowed his eyes in the Pechenih manner and turned coldly away. They were nothing to him.

Always in late summer the Pechenihs moved closer to the Dnipro with their flocks and herds. Not that the pasture land thereabout was much to speak of. On the contrary. But the other spoils were good—were excellent, in fact. For, late in summer, the Northmen of Scandia and the Kievan and Novhorodian merchant-warriors began returning home from their summer's marauding, and from their trading expeditions across the sea to Byzantium, where stood proud Tsarhorod, city of fabled splendor, of riches undreamed of—queen city of the world. So the Pechenihs heard it spoken of and spoke of it among themselves, their thin lips slavering at the mere thought of the plunder that came their way from it.

The merchant-warriors sailed the homeward way in boats laden to the guards with lengths of Byzantine silks and brocades, amphorae of wine, unheard of fruits, glass beads and bracelets for every woman, precious stones for the rich, caskets filled with the spices and scents of Araby, and slaves from the wide world over. All of which they had traded for the rich furs of animals trapped in the distant forests of the north, for barrels of honey and big round cakes of beeswax, and for slaves.

For the Pechenihs it was always an exciting, opulent time. Reaching the river, some remained at the

41

broad shallow that lay below the seven cataracts, where the merchants' men had to hoist their ships onto their shoulders for portage past it. Others moved on to the fourth of the cataracts, the most precipitous and wildest of them. Here, within its sound, the Pechenih raiders pitched their tents. And they waited.

They had never long to wait, for at this season of the year, until snow flew, hardly a day passed without the appearance of a merchant's flotilla. Here the merchants' men, beaching their ships and disembarking, worried them onto logs that were kept there for the purpose, then dragged them past the pounding, foaming, roaring waters.

Their ordeal was uphill. And, struggling thus with their boats, they made ready prey for the nomads.

Of course the merchants did not come to this slaughter innocent as babes. They traveled well armed with war hatchet, with bow and arrow, with a knife in the boot and spear ready at hand. And they counted among their number some of the best warriors in the world. For, many of them were Northmen, feared the wide world over for their skill in battle, as they were renowned for their luck in seamanship, in trading and raiding. Nevertheless, more often than not the Pechenihs returned to camp laden with plunder and dragging captives.

Bern easily recalled those wildly merry times in the Pechenih camps. Women and girls came running with shrieks of delight. Soon, many a one was decked in foreign finery. Favored girls and women appeared swathed in precious colored silks, which they wrapped right over the rags of last season. Dragged in the dirt and snagged on steppe grass, the silks turned to tatters within a week. The humblest woman of the tribe went hung about with gewgaws.

And every chief's tent had new chalices of silver, gold plate, caskets brimful of exotic pepper, fruits with names unknown.

Joining in the excitement, the dogs for their part ringed the day's captives and barked without cease. The women peered at the captives, poked and felt of them, laughing and chattering happily all the while. Whenever Bern thought of this, and that was seldom, he supposed that once he and his mother had stood thus.

After every raid the amphorae of princely wine were quickly emptied at the revels that always followed, with dancing, with brawling and feasting till one retched at the mere thought of food or drink.

In the darkness, remembering, Bern let out a little sigh.

Well, to get back to the journey upriver, Long Face had had to tie Bern up, hand and foot, to prevent his escape back into the steppe. But in a few days, after a short, harsh lesson in rowing punctuated by cuffs and lashes, he was put to work at one of the oars.

Bern minded neither the cuffs nor the work. What he regretted and brooded over was that at some time during the fight he had lost his cap. Without it, he felt strangely defenseless, exposed to every harm.

In the fleet were a score of boats, with fifty or so men to each. At night, they cast anchor and built their supper fires on the narrow, sandy shore. Each crew built its own, so that twenty fires were strung along the beach, flickering in the night.

On Bern's ship there were a few who had been wounded during the fight with the Pechenihs. These were nightly carried out on the beach and their needs attended to by their comrades. When the men had finished eating, they sat talking of trading or battle, of ships they had known and voyages they had gone on. Sometimes—another entertainment—two or three might come to friendly blows. Always, beside every campfire at least one game of knucklebones was in progress.

Almost every night the men danced and sang. They sang in the boats, too, during the days. They were a singing people. Sometimes a song stirred something in Bern, too vague for a memory, yet real enough to make him believe that he had heard those very sounds before—at some time, somewhere.

At first Bern was shackled by one ankle to his rowing bench. Someone would bring him a wooden bowl of hot gruel. Usually there was also a bit of fish fresh caught and boiled over the camp fire.

By night Bern was so wearied by the day's rowing that, having gulped the last of the gruel and licked the bowl and his fingers of every speck of flavor, he let the bowl slip from his hand and lay down on the bench. Unmindful of the stink of the bilge sloshing about in the bottom of the boat, he slept the night through till he was prodded awake again before day-break.

Now and again one of the men came up to him and spoke something in an asking tone of voice. Bern did not wholly understand the words but he knew again the cadence of the speech. For several days after his capture, however, he made no answer

44

except with sullen eyes. But one day the merchant chief himself came up to him and asked something. And something in the sound or perhaps the tone of his voice stirred a memory in Bern. It did not seem to be in his head but elsewhere within him. He looked up at the man and without entirely willing it uttered the words, "I am called Bern, son of Mikula."

At that the merchant and his aide began talking animatedly back and forth. After that, more of the men came to Bern and spoke to him. But he did not answer them and through the rest of the voyage spoke scarcely another word.

He lost count of the days of the journey upriver. Eight? Nine? It seemed a month of days! And with each day the river narrowed. On the left bank, the boundless steppeland, its distant horizon beckoning to the far away, was left behind. Now the land along that bank was darkened with forests, black, morose and brooding. The men never put in on that shore, never camped there. It seemed empty of people . . .

Here, since there was no longer danger of Bern's escaping back to the Pechenihs, Long Face took the shackle from his leg.

The opposite bank was a high bluff nearly all the way, with only a narrow strip of beach here and there. Bern's oar was on that, the portside. Now and again on the top of the bluff he could see clusters of huts.

Once he even saw people standing on the edge of the bluff, motionless, staring in their direction. Unable to take his eyes away, Bern stared back until his eyes watered, for it was from such a settlement (perhaps even this very one!) that his mother and he had been captured. For, though rarely, the Pechenihs did sometimes go raiding among the hamlets—but more for the lark of it than for plunder. For, what booty, besides a basket of grain and a captive or two, does the husbandman yield?

At night Bern was alone aboard ship, for the men all slept around their campfires. By now the rowing no longer wearied him as before and since he was unshackled, he passed the time till dark exploring the vessel. He came to know it as intimately as he later knew Long Face's hut.

Till then, he had seen such boats only from shore, as he stood with the Pechenihs watching fleets of them journeying up and down river. Even at a glance one could tell that those ships were built by a special breed of men. The Pechenihs, horsemen and herdsmen that they were, never built anything more than crude and flimsy rafts. But these ships were stoutly built of oak timbers skillfully planed with the ax and cunningly fastened together with wooden pegs. Though sturdy, yet they were trim, and maneuvered as easily as a fish in the water.

On Bern's boat were fifteen oars to the side. But some of the boats, he had noticed, were shorter or longer. And so used were the men to the oar that only one or two trial strokes and all thirty were rowing in perfect unison, in perfect rhythm.

It was one early evening while Bern was thus poking about the ship that he made the great find. Purely out of curiosity, he had got down on his hands and knees to peer between some amphorae of wine stowed aft of the ship. And there, within arm's reach, he saw a dark splotch. He stared at it a moment and

46

when it did not move, he stretched out his hand, touched something soft, then drew it out.

To his surprise, to his joy, it turned out to be a Pechenih cap, evidently left behind during the raid and kicked aside. With a smile on his face, he turned it about in his hands. Then he put it on his head.

It fit perfectly! And it seemed to him that that cap had been waiting for precisely himself to find it.

That night, as Bern lay in the boat watching the darkening sky and the stars igniting one by one, he tried to imagine himself back on the steppe with the Pechenihs. And he very nearly succeeded.

The next morning, the men first stared, then pointed and laughed at the cap atop Bern's head. But they made no move to take it away from him. And that was well.

That day, more than a fortnight after his capture, Bern sensed a special excitement among the men as they prepared to weigh anchor that morning. With special eagerness they came leaping into the boat, went for their oars, and rowed as they had not rowed before. One word in particular was on everyone's lips. Kiev.

On and on they rowed, till at last, when the sun had passed somewhat beyond the top of the sky, they rounded a bend. Then, seemingly by common consent, they shipped their oars. As one, all faces were turned to portside and all eyes gazed toward the top of the bluff.

In the total silence, Bern, too, stared. On the top of the bluff, on a point overlooking the river, stood what seemed to be a city. It was walled even along the steep river side, so that nothing of it could be seen but a few towers and a cluster of domes above which something glittered. Here and there, from pinnacles within the walls, bright pennants fluttered in the breeze.

After that long, silent moment, a hoarse shout went up from the men. Eagerly they took to their oars again and feverishly they rowed. By hard work athwart the current at last they drew near a large forested spit of land directly below the city. Veering shoreward, one by one the entire flotilla maneuvered its way into a sizable harbor.

The harbor area was thronged with people. From the height of the bluff, along a road that led to the harbor, Bern could see other people hurrying down. Most of the crowd was composed of women, some with children in arms. Shouts and cries rose on every side as the men leaped ashore, seized women by the waist and plucked up children.

As Bern leaped out of the boat after Long Face, he was filled with a nameless, almost unbearable excitement. He stood rooted in the midst of the throng, gazing at the scene. All around him were laughing women claiming their husbands, joyous shouts from the voyagers returned as they claimed their wives and children. In the happy confusion, for once no eyes were on Bern. He could have slipped away unnoticed.

Afterwards, whenever he thought of that day—and that was seldom, but sometimes it grew too big in his thoughts for him to put away—whenever he thought of it, the most painful part to remember was this, that no one came to claim him.

So much for the annals of Bern till that moment. The rest was short enough. The next day Long Face

thrust a thing he called a hackleboard under his nose and gave him a brief lesson in hackling bast. From that day on bast was the substance of Bern's life as from dawn to dusk he bent over the hackleboard or turned the spinning wheel for Long Face.

And now here had come a new turn in Bern's life. And he was sure that nothing he could do or attempted to do would change matters an iota. For his fate was the will of Allah, as some Pechenihs would say. So best let happen what would. Having learned this early, Bern had lived almost his whole life in this impassive manner.

He remembered how some of the captives among the Pechenihs had sickened and pined away because of having been torn from their native place. Fortunately, however, this would not happen to him, for he knew no native place. So in him there was none of that passion.

A metallic sound at the door of the kiln hut brought Bern on the instant back to where he lay. Someone was lifting the pin from the hasp. It might be Elek, bringing him breakfast. Bern sat up and waited, his eyes squinted against the blaze of sudden light that was coming.

There was no need for the lock. Even if he had the will to run away, he did not have the courage.

 In the next few days Bern came to understand that almost his sole task from now on would be the kneading and refinement of the clay. If he had known this, he would not have applied himself to it with such a will at the first.

At Long Face's, when he had been at work hackling bast, his hands cut and festering sometimes, he used to think that it surely must be the most painful and tedious of tasks, and that almost any other would be easier.

But refining clay, he found, had its own hardships. His arms and legs soon tired of pounding and kneading the clay. Yet if he paused for too long at a time the master noticed and at once inquired what the matter was. By dusk Bern was numbed by the dullness of his day's work. Even at night he could not escape it, for the smell of clay was on his hands and the taste of it in his mouth.

And, as if all this were not enough, Bern soon learned that here was a master hard to please. If, in shaping the refined clay into tiles he found the tiniest pebble in it that Bern had overlooked or not bothered to pluck out, he spoke loudly of it, in such terms that one would have thought it a boulder, no less.

Bern wondered at these exacting demands that the master made upon him in the work, and not only upon him but upon Elek as well. But most puzzling of all was his making the same demands of perfection upon himself, for all that he was the master.

No doubt worse could have happened to Bern. He tried to keep this toward the fore of his thoughts during the nights as he lay in the dark, listening to the voices coming through the wall between the kiln hut and the dwelling. Though the wall seemed stout enough, he found that he could hear much of what was said on the other side of it, especially if they were sitting at table. The mistress' voice came through especially clearly.

Lying on his sheepskin, his hands behind his head, Bern could listen in comfort, without the obligation of having to contribute anything to the talk. Or, if he preferred, he could stop listening and turn to his own thoughts. It was a little like sitting with the Pechenihs around their campfires, for there, too, he had listened all he pleased, but without making comment.

He came to think of the wall as a friend of sorts, equal with the dark, and equally undemanding of him.

Now and again he even heard himself mentioned. On those occasions he sat up at once and pricked up his ears. But the talk about him was usually brief and incidental to discussion of the master's work.

Much of the talk turned on affairs outside the hut. The mistress especially, after her daily trip to the well in the lane, could be depended upon to bring home tidbits of news or gossip. "While I was drawing water this morning," she would say, "I stopped to chat for a moment with our neighbor Sofronia—and guess what she told me."

"Give up!" the master would say at once.

Then the mistress would launch into a lengthy and wordy account of some event, often trivial, and usually so intricate that Bern's head was set awhirl with names of people unknown to him, obscure references to events of years before, statements begun but not finished, and false beginnings, all to the accompaniment of exclamations of surprise, indignation, scorn, amusement and the like that the master rather absentmindedly but steadily supplied.

Nevertheless, in this way Bern managed to piece together a story of nearly everybody in the lane. He learned also that the name of the youth they had met while digging clay was Yan and that he and Elek were indeed good friends. Yan, furthermore, was the chosen leader of the youths in the lane.

If the well was a source of news in the potters' lane, the market in the city, it seemed, yielded news from the larger sphere of Kiev. "While I was at market today," the mistress would begin, "I met with our kinswoman Svani, and you'll never believe what she told me!"

As often as not, the news concerned the Great Princess Olha. The Princess, old though she was, and almost recluse now, still gave her people much to talk about—if one took the master and his family for example. She seemed to be a favorite topic with them and much of what they said about her had the flavor of legend—at least, so it seemed to Bern.

"I remember the time some dozen years ago," the master began one night, "when Olha journeyed to

Tsarhorod to visit the Greek emperor. I was already grown by then and was in the crowd that stood on the heights watching them all embark and sail away. Mind you, eighteen court ladies accompanied our Princess—or so they say—not to speak of twelve ladies-in-waiting, and these besides the boyars, the forty-two merchants, the twenty ambassadors and all their wives and who not else with their wives. And I haven't even mentioned the servants—several to each person. Hoo! What pomp and pageantry!"

"I've often heard it said," the mistress put in, "that she acquitted herself well with the Greeks, that their emperor was taken with her great beauty and that he marveled at her wit and her wisdom. Yet, sometimes I wonder what wisdom there was in her becoming a Christian."

Bern listened carefully. Though he had heard of Christians, to his knowledge never had he seen one. Judging from remarks on the other side of the wall, Kiyans were not much attracted to the new belief of their Princess. "Will this God of hers bring us better luck than our old gods?" the mistress said. "Just ask yourself that! And what's to do," she went on, her voice rising, "if the one God fails to bring luck? Hm? What then—with no other god to turn to?"

"True, wife, true," the master agreed. "For all her wisdom, the old Princess seems not to have thought of that. Yet, we Kiyans can all be thankful that she has not pressed the new belief on us, as she might well have done, but left us to our own."

"Yes, but," here Elek spoke up, "didn't she urge it on Sviatoslau?"

"True. But don't forget that he had the good sense

54

to decline to follow his mother's footsteps."

"Akh! That Sviatoslau!" the mistress' voice broke in, indignant now. "What sort of son is that? Just tell me! Always absent on campaigns, and in lands so distant that not even the cock's crow reaches them!"

"Well—true," the master agreed reluctantly. "He does seem ridden by some grand scheme of conquest. Perhaps he cannot find rest from it."

"Rest?" the mistress protested. "And what sort of rest does the poor old Princess get? I say that Sviatoslau ought to bide at home, look after our affairs like a proper prince, look after his old mother like a proper son, and take the burden from those bowed shoulders."

"All the same," Elek broke in again, "I love him well, that Sviatoslau!"

"There! You see? Now what sort of model is that for our youngsters?"

"But he's a brave one, for all that, mother! You can't deny that!"

"There's that song the bards sing about him in the market place," the master put in. "How does it go? 'He steps light as the leopard on his campaigns. He scorns the soft pallet—' "

" '—and sleeps on the ground head pillowed on saddle,' " Elek chimed in. "And then there's the refrain: 'Stand firm, my comrades, stand firm! And I will go before!' "

All this talk served further to whet Bern's desire to see the city, to see for himself at least the biding place of these lofty beings already legendary though yet alive. Bern heaved a deep sigh. He might very well live and die under the very walls of the city and

55

never step foot within it.

The fact that the Great Princess Olha was one of those rare beings, a Christian, was astonishing enough. But the most astonishing thing Bern learned about her was that during the long years of her son's nonage as well as during his absences, she ruled the land in his stead.

At first Bern thought he had not heard aright. As if in response to his bewilderment, on the other side of the wall the mistress continued the conversation, saying to Elek, "And don't think that she was a mere figurehead, my son."

The master snorted with amusement. "Ho! Not that one!" he cried. "In her young days, after her husband's death, she traveled up and down the land seeing to affairs. Where she could make improvement, she made it. She holds our affairs in strong hands and we can be thankful for that."

"Ah, me!" the mistress gave a long sigh. "I doubt that we Kiyans have a like ruler in that Sviatoslau, for all that he's her son!"

"And yet, wife, don't forget that other side of her nature . . ." The master spoke thoughtfully.

"What other side? What other side?"

"Why, witness, for one, her vengeful war against the Derevlians, who murdered her husband . . ."

An exclamation of pique came from the mistress. "If," she retorted, "one is to believe all that one hears! But it only proves that she can deal not only with the crafty Greeks but also with the likes of the Derevlians in their dark forests up there to the north. And you call it vengeful, but I call it looking out for one's own interests. You have not heard a peep out of the Derevlians—have you? Not in all these years! It might have been otherwise if she had merely wrung her hands over her husband's murder. And we Kiyans, too, might at length have suffered at their hands, don't forget!"

"Well, well, wife, I meant no harm. Long life to her, I say!"

A pause, then, "But to bed! To bed!"

Of nights as he lay on the sheepskin, Bern listened to all this talk and pondered it before he fell asleep. He wondered especially about the Princess, not knowing what to think of her. For among the Pechenihs women were—women. They were good for fetching, carrying, cooking, and the dozens of other tasks of daily living.

But—ruling? Not even a Pechenih chief's wives were deemed anything more than ordinary women. How different from the Princess Olha! For that matter, how different from the mistress! "Looking out for her own interests," the mistress had said of the Princess.

But was that even womanly, to be so bold and forward? Bern puzzled long over this.

Sometimes his thoughts of the Princess Olha shifted imperceptibly to thoughts of his own mother. Though he had long ago ceased to think about her, except fleetingly at times, now he sometimes lay in the dark trying hard and persistently to remember all that he could about her. In the end, he always had to give it up. His mother remained in his memory almost entirely only as a feeling, and vague at that. He could not remember what she looked like, nor the sound of her voice, though she had been the one who had taught him to say in their own tongue, "I am called Bern, son of Mikula."

One night Bern had such a jumbled dream that though afterwards he remembered it with sharp clarity, he could make nothing of it. In the dream the mistress appeared, flourishing the wooden mallet that he used to pound the clay and shrieking, "Off with his head! Off with his cap!"

Then, before he knew it, she was not the mistress but the Princess Olha. Bern somehow knew her to be the Princess for all that he had never laid eyes on her. She sat gazing at him seriously, with anxious eyes, as he repeated the words, "I am called Bern, son of Mikula."

The dream was so real that he woke and it seemed to him that he had uttered the words aloud, for they were still hovering in the air. Sometimes—in the worst of times—those words seemed like a talisman to Bern. In a curious way, that he could not begin to understand, the feel of them on his tongue filled him with a marvelous solace.

Not a week had passed at the new master's before Bern was dying of tedium from the monotony of his task. One morning he even awoke with the thought that he would be living out his days and perhaps even growing old over that monstrous tub. Perhaps Elek had spoken prophetically and he would indeed be kneading clay till very doomsday.

That morning the master, followed by Elek, came briskly in with a "Now, then!"

Bern, misunderstanding, jumped to his feet and started for the hateful tub. "No, no, leave that!" the master said curtly. "Today you'll have another task. Come over here."

When Bern had obediently stepped up to the table, the master pushed toward him the small stone mortar with the iron pestle in it that Bern had noticed on his very first day in the kiln hut. The master threw some hard lumps of blue stuff into the vessel and said, "Now, then, crush this enamel to powder."

Heartened by this unexpected relief, not to mention the change of scene, however slight, Bern sat down at the table and set to work. Now at last, without seeming to shirk his task, he could watch more closely than before what the master and Elek were about. And it seemed to him, too, that he had at last been permitted to join the two of them and that they made a trio as they worked.

Over most of the tables were spread the raw tiles that for several days past had been drying outdoors in the open air. Elek now scooped some brown powder out of a large vessel and sprinkled it liberally over each tile. As if he had noticed that Bern was watching him from under his brows, he said, "It's glaze. I've got green glaze and yellow, too."

That did not altogether answer Bern's curiosity, but, for fear he might be sent back to the refining tub, he ventured no questions. The master, almost as if he were dancing, stepped lightly to the kiln in the corner of the hut.

It stood on a raised hearth and, of course, was built of clay. Inside it were two compartments. That much Bern had already found out for himself. The lower compartment was apparently the firebox and the upper the oven into which the tiles were placed to bake. Beside it stood two wooden buckets heaped with charcoal.

"Go get a live coal from your mother, Elek," the master said as he began laying pieces of the charcoal in the firebox.

Elek left the hut and soon reappeared with some glowing coals on a small shovel. Carefully he placed them in the kiln and stood watching till the charcoal caught.

That done, the master began tending that fire as if it were a sacred one, no less. Time and again he got down on his knees and peered into the firebox, long poker in hand, and rearranged the glowing coals, heaping them or spreading them. Sometimes he added a few judicious chunks of charcoal from the bucket.

In between, he came over to Bern, pinched up some of the powdered enamel, thoughtfully rubbed it between his fingers, then without a word returned to the kiln. At last, on one of these occasions, he said, "Enough. Now grind me some of the green."

Though out of doors the wind blew cold that day, the heat from the kiln soon made it stifling indoors, even though the door was finally opened. Now the reason for the curious arrangement of having the workshop separate from the dwelling became plain to Bern. If the kiln threw off a stifling heat now, in chilly weather, what would it be like in midsummer?

At last, toward noon, the master declared the oven ready. Bern watched while he and Elek carried the raw tiles to the oven. But the master alone carefully laid them in.

That night Bern was given strict orders not to touch the fire, "else it will go badly for you," the master said, fixing him with an eye.

When the door was fastened shut for the night, the heat in the kiln hut soon became almost unbearable. In torment, Bern abandoned his sheepskin and moved into the corner farthest from the kiln. The clay floor, at least, was cool.

Several times that night the master came in to see to the kiln, leaving the door open while he did so. He came in the dark, without a rush light, guided, apparently, by the eye of the fire. Taking advantage of the opened door, Bern got up each time and gulped cold air while he could.

The next morning, after the fretful night, during which the lice, livened by the heat, had all but devoured him, he was aroused before dawn. "Up! Up!" the master cried.

This time he had a rush light, which he thrust on a spike jutting from the wall above the kiln. Blinking in the sudden light, Bern got slowly to his feet.

Elek came in. "Are they done?" he asked.

The master, peering into the kiln, said, "To a turn!" as if speaking of tarts baking in an oven.

Taking a long-handled flat wooden shovel that stood propped against the wall, he began lifting the tiles out of the oven and carrying them to the table. The glaze that Elek had besprinkled them with had melted and given each a shiny golden brown surface.

When the master had them all laid out, he began looking them over one by one. With a stick he pushed nearly every other one aside or right off the table to fall to the floor and break. Bern could see that some of these rejected tiles were cracked or bent or otherwise misshapen. And the glaze on some was unevenly coated. Yet some seemed perfect. A few fell to the floor bottom side up and Bern could see that they were impressed with the small round spiral that was the master's own mark.

Straightening at last, and noticing Bern looking on, the master gave him a look of satisfaction. "Good," he said. "Fewer spoiled than usual." For the first time that morning he smiled. "Maybe you've brought me luck, boy," he said to Bern.

Bern shrugged his shoulders diffidently. Good luck or bad luck—if it was another's, what did it matter to him?

At this moment the mistress came in with a bowl of gruel for Bern. Setting it down in front of him, she paused to glance at the new baked tiles for a moment and then silently went out. As soon as Bern finished eating he returned to the task of the day before, content that again he could observe the busy activity, however furtively.

By this time Elek had lit a fire in the brazier on the table. Now he took up one of the small vessels with two compartments within it. Sifting some of the fine green enamel into one of the compartments and some of the blue into the other, he set it on the brazier, which by now was glowing white hot.

In a little while the powder in the crucible had melted to liquid. Now with a pair of tongs the master picked it up and, slowly moving it back and forth over the hot tiles laid out on the table, poured the melted enamel onto them in the thinnest of streams, making a design on each tile. Depending upon how he tipped the crucible, he poured first one and then the other and sometimes even both colors at a time out of the pot.

At last he set it down, empty. Elek handed him an iron stylus and with its point the master began pulling some of the lines of liquid color on the tiles into new positions. The lines easily moved over the shiny, already hardening glaze of the tile. In this way he made a variety of designs.

All during this spectacle of skill, Bern, completely forgetting himself and the task before him, sat watching with mouth ajar. At last the master straightened his back. There were beads of sweat on his brow and the scar across his chin had turned a vivid red, as if it were a raw wound again. He glanced at Bern. "Don't gape," he said, "else a magpie will fly into your mouth."

Bern, coming to, resumed the grinding.

That night as he lay in the dark, idly Bern wondered about the master's curious passion for his work, his passion for perfection, as if making tiles were the most important matter in the world. And Elek, too, was obviously becoming infected with that same fever . . . Certainly no man among the Pechenihs was ruled by such passion for mere work—unless, of course, it had to do with horses or raiding.

 The morning after that short interval at the work table, Bern was back to kneading clay. But that day for the first time the door was kept open all the day long, for, however slowly, summer was coming on. Since Bern no longer needed to keep his eyes steadily on his work, he relieved the tedium by gazing out of doors. Over the top of the high wattle fence that enclosed the yard he had a tantalizing view of the wall of the city brooding over the potters' lane and above that a patch of the changing sky.

After that day, what with the warming sun, the door was usually kept open, so that Bern could watch the events out of doors as he worked. Now and again the mistress' flock of chickens, squired by their cock, strolled their way past, pecking and conversing privately among themselves. And one time he saw a pair of cranes, foraging for food, briefly join the flock.

One day the scene was further enlivened by the sudden appearance of a large cat on top of the fence. Poised there, it hesitated a moment, then half climbed, half leaped to the ground. Bern watched it come striding across the yard toward the kiln hut. To his contentment it came in through the door as bold as if it lived there.

First it rubbed its spine against the tub. Then it rose on its hind legs, put its front paws on the rim, and inspected the inside. Delicately it sniffed and then as delicately gave a sneeze.

At this, Elek turned. "Why, here's the cat come back!" he exclaimed.

"Now where have you been tramping about all this time, you minx?" the master said. "I suppose it doesn't matter to you that the mice have got completely out of hand."

Head and tail disdainfully aloft, the cat padded out.

It was that same day that, suddenly, Bern became aware that no sounds were coming from the river. Astonished, he paused and listened. The air was still. Could the ice have gone already? Reluctant, moody, he resumed his work.

During the lengthening days immediately following, the lane that he could not see came alive with the sunny sounds of spring—with laughter and young voices summoning the spring with song. From over the fence came the shouts of children at play, the banging of wooden buckets at the well, sometimes the shrill voices of women scolding or calling to their children. Now and again Bern caught a glimpse of the mistress going in or out through the gate, carrying buckets on a beam over her shoulders, or heard her voice greeting a neighbor. He could hear the screaking of the windlass on the marvelous well, and from the neighboring yards the intermittent whirring of the potters' wheels. Evidently they had moved their work

67

out of doors.

In spite of his limited view Bern could follow the progress of the approaching summer just from listening to the children. One day up the lane and down .they set up the bluejay's cry: "Viy, viy, take the wagon, stow the sleigh!"

Another day it was shrill cries of "Geese! Geese! Here's straw for your nest!"

And when Bern looked up he glimpsed a long skein of wild geese winging across the sky. But one day suddenly came whoops of "Stork! Stork! Nest on our hut! Nest on ours!"

And sure enough, in the next moment, wheeling in the sky above the lane a stork came into view. With that, the entire lane, up and down, was resounding with cries of "Stork! Stork! Nest on our hut!"

In the kiln hut, Elek suddenly dropped something with a clatter and went dashing out, his father not far behind him. Bern sat back on his heels, perplexed and not a little alarmed. In the next instant Elek came back, stuck his face in at the doorway, and shouted to Bern, "Come on! The storks! The storks are back!"

Then he dashed off again. Now the mistress could be seen hurrying across the yard, looking up, her hand shielding her eyes from the sunlight.

Bern stayed where he was. What did it matter to him that the storks were back?

But from that day a fever of restlessness, a terrible yearning gnawed at Bern. And time dragged so that each day seemed a week. Ceaselessly he longed for the out of doors, out there where the earth was greening. Longingly he gazed up at the city. But he would have been glad even to step out into the lane. He no longer welcomed the coming of dark and the end of the day's work. For that only meant being shut up in the kiln hut for the night.

He began to look back upon his life among the nomads who, toiling as little as possible, lived off their flocks and booty seized from others who toiled, as a paradise. He could not admit to himself that in fact it had been quite otherwise.

Here among the Kiyans there was simply no letup to industry. Bern could not see the sense of the ceaseless toil, of cooping oneself under a roof and wasting day after day in dull industry. He marveled that though Elek was not a captive yet even with no one to goad him he seemed content to keep to his tasks.

Yet, for all this, it never once occurred to Bern to try squirming out through the little window or somehow to break the hasp or the hinges of the door and make a bolt for freedom. For, there are some things even more dreadful than bondage.

But Bern was not without company. Usually there was the talk coming through the wall from the master's hut. Though he could not always make out the words and though in any case they were certainly not directed to him, still, just the sounds of the human voice were solace.

Often there was even laughter.

But one night something else presented itself. Bern was lying on his sheepskin on the hearth in front of the kiln, where he could hear the voices best, when he heard a slight sound from the direction of the door. He sat up and looked. Something was squeezing in through the gap under the door.

It looked like a large rat. Bern jumped to his feet. Without moving, he looked wildly about for a weapon. It had got into the room by now.

But instead of scurrying off, it came padding slowly toward Bern. "Meow," it said in greeting.

Bern doubled over in silent laughter.

The cat rubbed her back against his leg. He picked her up and sat down. When he drew her against his chest, he could feel her purring. Truly, she was purring! At last he lay down, the cat snuggled beside him, and to the sound of her loud, steady murmuring, he fell asleep. In the morning, when he woke, she was gone.

That day, as luck had it, there was a chicken wing in his bowl again. By heroic self-denial, Bern refrained from more than a nibble or two at it before hiding it away among the folds of his sheepskin where he kept his cap.

Then he could hardly wait for night. But at last night came and he continued to wait.

And wait.

And at last, when he thought he could no longer forebear eating the piece of chicken himself, the cat came.

Thereafter, when her night's hunt was done, she often squirmed her way into the kiln hut, accepted whatever tidbit Bern had to offer, and in return kept him company for a time.

But, when all's said, the cat was not the best of friends. Bern soon learned that she had her own purposes and try as he would he could not hold her when she did not want to stay. Free to come and to go, unlike himself, she moved in and out of the kiln hut as

70

whim dictated. Nor could she be shut up.

One night, to keep her in, Bern went so far as to stuff the sheepskin into the gap under the door. For the sake of the cat's companionship he was prepared to shiver through the chilly night without it.

But the cat would not have it that way. After trying passionately to dislodge the sheepskin and failing, she sat back and began to yowl, loud and mournful. Bern, completely surprised and puzzled by the animal's furious determination, had to let her go.

And in other ways the cat proved unsatisfactory as a friend. Though at night she made straight for Bern when she came, whenever she visited the kiln hut during the day she seemed not to regard him in any special way. She might or might not greet him first of all. In either case she greeted Elek and the master with precisely equal affection.

And those two, as likely as not, returned the greeting only by pushing her away with a foot, crying, "Tsur! Tsur! Be off!"

And then, quite unexpectedly one night, matters took a turn. As Bern lay in the kiln hut thinking of nothing, not even, as a matter of fact, listening to the voices his friend the wall was sending through to him, he suddenly heard his name spoken.

He sat up.

On the other side of the wall the master had spoken, saying, ". . . and take Bern with you."

"Very well, then," Elek replied. "We'll take the tiles to the city first thing in the morning."

Bern sat motionless, staring into the dark, scarcely daring to breathe. At last he lay down again, carefully. He wasn't going to let himself even think that he might not have heard aright.

It seemed to him that all that night through he did not sleep a wink for thinking of tomorrow's bright promise. Whether or no he slept, in the morning he awoke with spirits soaring.

9 Their pace was slow, for the baskets of tiles were heavy and by now they were climbing the steepest part of Borich's Wagon Road on their way to the city. Walking beside Elek, Bern thought back. Was it really only three weeks since he had climbed this road with Long Face? It seemed more like three months!

And what a change! The road was alive with carts and wagons creaking past them in both directions. Those going down were for the most part rattling empty. But those going up were filled with timbers, with fish, or barrels of salt. One cart was loaded with a pile of tanned cowhides, evidently being brought up from the tanners' quarter below.

A steady stream of people, some mounted, but most on foot, was also moving along the road. A few were still muffled in sheepskins—and in truth, there was still a lingering hint of chill in the air.

After a while Bern noticed that those approaching them looked at him with that certain curiosity on their faces. Of course, they were not looking at him but at the cap on his head. This stirred a feeling of importance in him, so unusual that it only added to his lightheadedness this fine early spring morning.

At last Elek stopped and set down his two baskets. As he stood flexing his hands to ease the strain in them, he turned about and looked toward the river. Glad for the rest, Bern did the same. Instead of the almost solid expanse of ice that had covered the river only a few weeks ago, now only small chunks were bobbing silently southward.

Elek suddenly pointed. "The ferry's working again!" he cried. "That's a sure sign of summer coming!"

Squinting his eyes against the morning sun, Bern watched the ferryboat plying its way among the little chunks of ice. "Where does it go?" he asked.

"See that patch of yellow sand on the opposite shore?" Elek pointed. "It goes there. There begins the twin road through the forest that leads to Pereiaslau." He glanced at Bern. "That's another of our cities," he added when he saw the question on Bern's face. "But Kiev is the chiefest, and our Prince rules over all."

He picked up his baskets and started on again. As Bern fell into step beside him, he was all the while savoring a feeling altogether new to him. It was the feeling of companionship. He stole a look at Elek. No doubt Elek would be amazed—or perhaps amused? —if he knew that Bern was even thinking of him as a possible friend.

They had reached the steepest part of the road. It hugged the bluff all along the way, so that only the wall of the city and nothing of what lay behind it was visible. But soon the city wall seemed to come to an end and along the edge of the bluff above them Bern saw a tall, imposing palisade built of matched timbers, just like that on Castle Hill. Elek nodded toward it. "Behind that is another of the princely palaces. It has a great hall built of stone."

Once past this palisade, the road began curving toward the right. In a few moments, at long last Bern, with Elek, gained the very top of the bluff on which the city stood. But, it now turned out, the city occupied only the forepart of the bluff, that overlooking the river. The rest was an immense open field dotted with hundreds of high, oblong mounds. Bern was so surprised to discover what lay behind the city that he halted.

"It's our burial ground," Elek explained, "and those are barrows. Some of them are very ancient." But he did not stop.

Soon they veered toward the right again, making straight toward a single barrow, the largest and highest by far of all those dotting the field. From behind it came a growing hubbub. "We're coming to the Old Women's Market," Elek said. "We have to pass through it to get to the city gate."

In the next moment, rounding the huge barrow, they came into an open space edged with huts and alive with people milling about. The air was filled with the bawling of venders crying their wares. Some stood behind stalls set up in front of the huts and between them. But most had their wares in baskets or spread out on the ground, which was paved with timbers.

Bern did not know what to look at first. Here was a fish stall; here baskets of dried mushrooms, herbs, and onions. Here were open sacks of golden millet. Next, crates of live chickens. Here was a grogshop, and next to it a stall with quarters of red meat hanging from iron hooks. Here was an ironmonger's stall hung with all kinds of cunning implements. Here were clay pots of every size and shape spread out on the ground. Here was a vender displaying, to the elbow on either arm, glass bracelets in a profusion of colors. Such a bewildering array of all manner of things! Bern had never seen the like.

But, careful to keep Elek's yellow head well in sight, he squirmed through the crowd after him. In odd corners he kept coming upon small groups of men or boys playing at knucklebones. It seemed to be a favorite game with Kiyans, at home and abroad!

At last, having worked their way through the noisy market, Bern and Elek reached the drawbridge in front of the gates of the city. Here, too, the way was slow, for the gates were too narrow for the crowds passing in and out. As Bern moved along, propelled as much by the crowd as by his legs, he stared up at the wall. It was made of clay heaped to an enormous height and hard packed. By now, even at a hundred paces, he knew clay when he saw it! The roofed battlement all along the top of it was built of timbers, with long horizontal slits just under the eave of the roof. Square towers on the battlement flanked the gate.

The drawbridge spanned a ditch that ran along the foot of the wall, so deep and steep that it made Bern dizzy just to look down into it. As they passed through the gate in the thick wall, the dank, dark smell of wet earth and wet wood overpowered the smell of the people among whom they were wedged. But suddenly they were in sunshine again, on a broad avenue paved with timber.

They were in the city at last.

In midstream of the people eddying around them, they set down their baskets to rest for a moment. In the past, whenever Bern indulged in his longing to see the city, he imagined that if ever that good luck came his way, he would simply burst with excitement. Instead, now that here at least he was standing within the city, he felt only a curious numbness and even a remoteness, as if all this were happening to some other person.

Judging by the air of purpose with which people moved, everyone had some definite errand as his goal. Bern stood, marveling at the number of errands that needed doing in the city.

Along the crooked lanes log huts stood thick as tents in a Pechenih camp, each behind its ragged paling of withes. Some dwellings, Bern noticed, even abutted the inner side of the city wall and stalls had been set up between some of them. Here and there, behind grand palisades of timbers, stood dwellings of the rich, two or even three times taller than the huts.

When, finally, Elek picked up his baskets and started on again, Bern took care to walk close beside him. Though their way was paved they crossed little lanes that, unpaved, were deep with the mud of spring thaw. Unknown to himself, a smile lit Bern's face as he looked about. For, tucked away among these little lanes and bypaths must be things to be discovered— some day.

Evidently proud that his city was making such an obvious impression on Bern, Elek began pointing out first one thing, then another. Straight ahead stood yet another princely castle, but this one without a palisade.

Bern stared at it. To him it did not seem to be a dwelling, for, built of stone, it was twice as tall as a hut and at the center rose a tower even taller. The tower was square, with a tentlike roof that glittered in the sun. Midway of its height an open gallery ran all along its front and sides. A banner fluttered from its peak.

But Elek was already pointing out other things. Down that lane over there to the left lived some kinfolk of theirs. Over there beyond the castle was the princely bathhouse. The large structures near it were the princely storehouses and various offices. That small one was the Princess' chapel. Over there—Bern was so busy looking that he forgot even the weight of the baskets and was only vaguely aware that they were all but pulling his arms out of their sockets by now.

At the same time, underneath all that, he was breathless with the heady sense of the new companionship he seemed to be sharing with Elek.

And then, suddenly, Bern saw them—the cluster of domes he had known so long. So unexpectedly did they come into view that he drew in his breath with surprise.

Elek, noticing, smiled. "That's St. Sofia—the Princess' new church that's abuilding. That's where we're going."

In the next instant, before Bern could quite recover from his surprise and savor the sudden delight he felt, from behind them came the jingle of gear and the thud of horses' hoofs approaching at a trot on the wooden pavement. They hurried out of the way to the side of the road. There they stopped and watched as a contingent of men, each bearing a lance, rode by, their shields slung over their backs. Each was helmeted and some wore shirts of mail. At their fore, resplendent in helmet and breastplate, rode a single horseman, mounted on a grey stallion. "That's the commander Pretich," Elek said, "and those are the Princess' guardsmen."

As Bern and Elek stood in the crowd watching, from behind them came a shout. "Hey! Elek!"

They both turned. Working his way toward them through the crowd, came Yan, the youth they had met at the clay diggings three weeks before. "Yan!" Elek cried. "What are you doing in town?"

Reaching them, Yan nodded at Bern and then said to Elek, "I had to bring some pots to market and just as I started for home, the Princess' guard came along. So I followed them in."

As Bern listened to the two friends talking back and forth, evidently no longer aware of him, he felt his new sense of companionship, scarcely yet savored, rapidly ebbing. He wanted to clutch for it, to keep it from escaping. But as well clutch at flowing water . . .

As they stood in the crowd, Elek and Yan began exchanging their favorites among the horses passing by. "I'll take that grey one of Pretich's every time," Elek said.

"As for me," Yan countered, "give me this bay that's just coming along."

Now if there was one thing that Bern knew better than anything and better than these two, it was horses. Not for nothing had he lived among the Pechenihs! Carried away with this thought, he burst out, "Akh! Those two are nothing—all show and little else!" He pointed to a small mount just passing by them, with an unpretentious, rather shaggy coat of grey. "I'll take that one above all the rest! Watch its gait. It's a runner and if—"

He stopped, suddenly aware that Elek and Yan were not looking at him as he spoke, but at each other. Bern saw amused expressions on their faces, as if to say, "But who asked him?"

So, at any rate, he read those looks. With raucous, ringing cries a flock of rooks, startled by something, suddenly rose from the castle tower. Bern looked up at them without seeing them.

He had been building castles in the air.

 Ahead of them the long familiar cluster of domes rose to the sky. As Bern walked along beside Elek, keeping his eyes steadily upon them, he forgot all else. Though they were of different sizes and heights, they were all shaped like giant drops of water falling elongated and slightly bulbous at the bottom. Out of them sprang the slender golden crosses, each with two crossbars.

As they approached, Bern felt as if here at last he was coming to old friends, for he had known those domes from the very first day of his arrival in Kiev, before he had even set foot on its soil.

And how many of them were there? Walking along, he began to count. He got as far as ten. Yet there were more, he knew. But as he counted, the domes seemed mysteriously to shift, so that it seemed to him that he had missed some on the first try.

He began again. And again they seemed to shift, but so subtly that while he was busy counting one portion of them, more and more that he had missed seemed to be presenting themselves to view. Sooner count a flock of sheep moving across the steppe! He began again.

Suddenly Elek, though weighted by the heavy baskets of tiles, broke into an awkward run toward the church. From various directions other people were hurrying toward it. Bern left off trying to count the domes and followed as fast as he could. Reaching the church, he found Elek in the little crowd that had gathered in front of it.

The mounted guardsmen they had just been watching with Yan were ranged in front of the portico of the church. Almost hidden by them, on the ground stood a large, thronelike chair, canopied with some rich fabric and set on a platform from which four long handles projected. Beside each handle stood a man.

Elek set down his baskets. "The Princess must be coming out of the church!" he whispered.

The Princess! Unbelieving, Bern stared at the door under the portico of the church. It was closed. "Will she come through that door?" he whispered.

Elek nodded.

Bern shifted his gaze to the guardsmen. The commander Pretich was nowhere in sight. The guardsmen were standing about with reins slack, with lances atilt every which way, and some had their helmets off. Almost to a man they were golden haired and ruddy faced—and some even had a thatch of hair that blazed red as the sun. Bern had never seen such men.

"Who are they?" he whispered.

"The guardsmen, you mean?" Elek said. "They're Variahs—Norsemen in the princely service."

The little crowd of people stood quietly talking among themselves. Bern looked up at the church. He saw now that it was built entirely of wood, in clusters of chambers of different sizes and heights all joined together to make the single structure. And so monumental it was that Bern marveled that anyone could have built it. For one thing, had they used ladders to get so high? For another thing, how had they built those gently rounded domes out of straight pieces of wood? And who had been so fearless as to affix the crosses atop the domes?

Elek gave him a nudge in the ribs. Bern looked and saw that the guardsmen were putting their helmets back on, tightening hold of their reins, and coming to attention.

In the shadows of the portico, the church door had begun to open. A hush fell over the crowd as two men came out and took their stand on either side of the door. Staring silently through the doorway, the people waited. After a long moment, within the dim depths of the interior, the tall figure of a woman appeared. Slowly she moved toward them, her long mantle glinting faintly.

At last, reaching the doorway, the Princess came into full view. Her head was swathed in some sort of thin material intricately folded and draped, so that only her face was visible. She paused and gazed at the people and the people, hushed, gazed back.

At first Bern saw only the great dark eyes and the strong, black brows above them, which, instead of arching, ran long and straight and only near the ends bent sharply downward. Then Bern saw the mouth, full and generous enough, but held straight and firm in a severe line.

"She must be very old," the thought kept repeating itself in his head.

Just behind the Princess came the commander Pretich. At her either elbow appeared a guardsman. But

in the next instant, as at some signal, they moved back a pace and the Princess stepped out over the threshold alone. At this, the crowd, as if it had been holding its breath as one, let out a long, soft sigh.

Slowly the Princess moved across the portico down the few steps and toward the waiting chair. The guardsmen hovered at her elbows, but did not venture to touch her person.

Having reached the chair at last, she was helped—almost lifted—into it. Now her ladies came hurrying forward. Two adjusted her gown and mantle. Two more then laid a large coverlet of black fur over her knees. At last they stepped away. As one, the four men at the handles stooped and lifted the chair. Slowly, surrounded by the mounted men, they moved forward. At a seemly distance some of the crowd followed.

"Where is she going?" Bern whispered.

Some woman standing in front of him turned around and answered him, "Why, back to her stone palace on Castle Hill, no doubt. That's her favorite place nowadays."

Then the woman noticed Bern's cap. "Are you a foreigner, then?" she asked.

Fortunately, the crowd moved the woman away from Bern, saving him from having to think of an answer.

He picked up his baskets and followed Elek, who was already going into the church. Inside, he found himself in the largest and loftiest chamber he had ever seen. Straight ahead, sunlight streamed through an immense screen with numerous little openings and, at its center, a wide doorway through which Bern could see a smaller sunlit space beyond.

Along part of each side of the chamber ran a gallery edged with a parapet and supported by a series of arches and columns. The archways seemed to lead on into other chambers.

Out of the shadows under the gallery to the right a man of burly build, with a great broad torso set on a pair of long, sturdy legs, came toward them. Though he was clean shaven, his jowls were blue with beard already pushing out. Stuck in the belt of his none too clean tunic was a roll of parchment. "Well!" he said, sending his voice echoing through the chamber. "The tiles at last!" He peered into the baskets. "But is this all?"

"We'll bring more at once," Elek replied.

"At once," the man repeated. "What would that mean? Just now the Princess wanted to know when the tiling of the floor would be finished."

"We'll bring more today," Elek answered. "My father wishes me to say that now that he has a helper to refine the clay he will be able to provide the tiles you need more quickly."

The man glanced at Bern, then shifted his gaze to his hat. "Is this the helper? And what sort of gear is that you have on your head?"

Elek answered for him. "My uncle captured him from the Pechenihs. But he's one of ours."

"One of ours, is he?" The man looked at Bern. "How, then, did you fall among the Pechenihs? Eh?"

This time Elek did not come to his rescue, so Bern murmured his answer. The man kept his blue eyes on him for a long moment without saying anything. Then, pursing his lips, he shook his head ruefully.

Turning, he waved his big hand toward the screen. "Unload the tiles over there in front of the altar," he said to Bern. "That's where the tiler and his men will soon be working. And you, Elek, my boy, come with me. I have something to show you of further work." And he led the way in under the gallery.

Bern lugged the baskets over to the screen. He saw now that it was made of wood, and carved all over with leaves and vines, with rosettes and fish and crosses. For a long time Bern stood staring at it, trying to follow each design where it led. But at a sound behind him, he came to and began emptying the baskets and stacking the tiles.

When he had finished, he peeped through the large doorway in the screen. A long, rather high table stood there, but it was empty. Part of the floor in front of it was imbedded with a myriad of tiny, many colored square stones or some such substance, all fitted precisely together in such a way as to make a pattern. Set around the edges of this pattern were larger pieces, very much like the tiles the master made. Yes, he recognized some of the designs on the tiles and their colors as well. Evidently the work of tiling the floor was only just begun.

Looking up to the source of the light that flooded the space, Bern found himself gazing into the vault of one of the domes, perhaps the largest of the cluster. All around the base of it, like a necklet, was a series of openings. Moving his gaze downward, along the smooth, white wall behind the altar, for the first time Bern noticed that it was scrawled all over, from top to bottom, with black lines. They seemed to to be made by charcoal.

From behind him the burly man's voice suddenly spoke. Bern had been so rapt that he had not heard him coming. "Does it please you?" the man asked.

"Yes, I can see by your face that it does."

Bern did not smile, but he knew that his face spoke the wonder in him.

Elek asked, "Where will the Princess stand when she comes here to do her god honor?"

The man gave him a look. "Not 'her god' but God, since there is but one," he said. He waved a hand toward the gallery on the left. "Up there, with her waiting women. And down here all the others. And there on the altar will be the sanctuary. But go along now —both of you. I have work to do."

As soon as they were out of doors and out of earshot, Bern, still overwhelmed with wonder, asked, "Who is he?"

"You mean old Zhdan? He is our Princess' master builder." Elek tossed his head by way of indicating the church they were leaving behind them. "He's building St. Sofia, for instance, and he built the church in Vyshhorod and—"

"By himself?" Bern asked.

"Of course not by himself!" Elek laughed. "But he drew the plans and members of the carpenters' guild helped him build it. He's their elder, you see. They build bridges and fortifications, too." Elek paused, then added with wonder in his own voice, "And Zhdan knows numbers. He has to, to do his work. And he doesn't lack for that, I can tell you, for by our Princess' command there's always something abuilding in Kiev or in Vyshhorod."

"Vyshhorod?"

"Yes. Vyshhorod. That's the Princess' own city half a day's journey from here. My father made the tiles for the church she had built there. But it's not nearly as grand as this one."

That day Bern and Elek lugged eight more baskets of tiles to the church in the citadel. Bern wanted to linger, to wander about and see more of the church. But there was no such thought in Elek's mind. They hurried home for more tiles.

On their third and last arrival, in place of Zhdan, they were met by a youth, not much older than they, who talked briefly with Elek and oversaw them unloading the tiles.

"That was Kari, Zhdan's apprentice," Elek said on the way home.

"Apprentice?" Bern said.

"Akh, you don't know anything, do you?" Elek replied with a laugh. "He helps Zhdan and is learning to be a builder. For instance, I'm my father's apprentice. Some day I'll be a tilemaker, too."

On the way home at the end of that day Bern pondered the fact that among the Pechenihs no structures were ever built. For them, tents were not only sufficient but also necessary to their roaming life. The tents could be easily struck by the women whenever their flocks of sheep and herds of horses and cattle had eaten all the steppe grass within easy distance and it was time to move on to new pastures.

And that was another difference. Among the Pechenihs the women did all sorts of things. They not only fetched the water, built the fires, slaughtered the meat animals, cooked, saw to the young children and the flocks, but also sewed the tents and the clothing.

But as for the men, horsemanship and bowmanship were their only skills, and whatever goods they had were gained by raiding and barter. When they were not away on raids or bartering goods, they sat around the campfires drinking kumis, telling endless stories, and fashioning bows and arrows. They varied this monotony with breaking in new horses and with riding games and contests.

But as for building, they did not build. Among the Pechenihs there was never any question of what a man might do or be. But here in Kiev one was a rope maker, another a shipbuilder, still another a tilemaker, or—Bern glanced back toward the domes of St. Sofia for a final look—a builder of grand edifices. And as Bern thought of these differences, for the first time by comparison the Pechenih came off the worse.

That night, as if to top off this momentous day with luxury, a piece of meat came with his supper. He saved none of it for the cat, but ate it all himself.

Afterwards, locked in as usual, Bern lay on the sheepskin cozily listening to the talk on the other side of the wall. Elek was telling his parents about their trips into the city that day. "And just as we got there this morning, the Princess came out of the church."

Then he went on to describe the incident. Bern frowned as he listened. Elek was conveying not anywhere near the excitement of it. If only Bern were on the other side of the wall, how much better he could tell it!

"As a youngster," the master began when Elek had done, "many's the time I used to see Olha start off on the hunt to one of her preserves, usually that one she still keeps across the river from us. Sometimes she'd be on horseback, with a hooded falcon upon her wrist. Sometimes she'd follow the chase in a sleigh. But nowadays, I suppose, the young men of her retinue go hunting without her."

"Ah, poor soul," the mistress murmured. "At her age . . ." Her voice trailed away into silence.

During that silence, Bern, too wakeful to sleep, turned his thoughts to the day just past. So much had happened that he scarcely knew what to savor first: the visits to the city—three, no less!—the glimpse of the Princess Olha, or—Zhdan and the church he had built. Yes, certainly his visits to the church were the most memorable events of that memorable day!

Suddenly Bern sat up, too excited by his growing thoughts to be still. Did Kari know how lucky he was? No, of course not.

Bern lay down again. In the future, he now determined, he would seize upon every chance to watch the work in the church going forward. The thought made him feel oddly exhilarated, as if something caged within him had been set free, like a bird.

But—there's a spoonful of tar in this sweet barrel of mead . . . There was, for example, the boy Yan.

Bern frowned into the darkness. How easily that one had pushed him aside and fallen in with Elek! As if of course he belonged. Well—some belonged and some didn't. And nothing on this precious earth could change that, for, as some among the Pechenihs would say, such is the will of Allah.

For all that each day more and more birds, navigating the skies by way of the Dnipro, came winging back to Kiev, each day it was still touch and go whether winter or summer would prevail. For old woman winter never gives up her hold on the land without a battle. And that year the battle between winter and the maiden that is summer continued for many a day before the outcome became clear.

One day, purely out of spite, old woman winter dumped a heap of heavy, wet snow upon the city. But the very next day the righteous Sun of summer at once began melting it away. Everywhere could be heard the dripping, trickling, chuckling sounds of streamlets of melting snow. Thus defeated at last, the old woman packed bag and baggage and left for good.

Now Kiyans walked gratefully in the warming sunshine, their faces turned toward the heavens. The first of the rains that year came on a morning in late April. Everyone in the household—Bern included—had to troop out and stand with faces upturned to receive this special blessing sent them down from the heavens.

One early evening while Bern was eating his supper, suddenly, from somewhere up the lane, came the sound of girls singing. He lifted his head and listened. In a moment, as if in answer, masculine voices broke in. Back and forth the voices sang. Elek, who was sitting at the work table, was also listening.

He grinned and looked over at Bern. "That's our young people in the lane. They'll be gathering every night now all the summer long."

"What for?" Bern asked.

Elek looked at him, astonishment in his eyes. "What for? What do you mean, what for? Why, to look each other over, of course, so's to decide which they'll marry!"

Almost every evening after that Bern listened raptly to the singing. Some times the songs were derisive and mocking, ending in shrieks of laughter. Other times they were plaintive and lingered soft on the air for a long time afterward.

Down in the harbor, with each day the simmer of activity was slowly rising to a boil as merchants' boats began arriving from the shipyards far to the north, around Novhorod. Vessels were being outfitted with oars from last year's ships, with rudders and sails, with anchors and ropes. Provisions were being assembled and loaded on for the long and perilous journey downriver, across the sea, and through the strait to Tsarhorod. The goods to be traded were being loaded and stowed away. All of this was reported by Long Face on the day he dropped in to sit with the master over a cup of mead.

With the lengthening days the master increased the work. For the demand for tiles grew almost overnight as the masters of the building arts began taking to their work again after the long, dark, and nearly idle days of winter. On days when Bern helped Elek carry tiles to the city he could hear the sounds of carpenters' hammers and hatchets ringing throughout the city.

For Bern the discovery that men need not all be confined to one and the same task was heartening. Not, on the other hand, that one could choose freely . . . Like a garment caught on thorns, his leaping thoughts were snagged and brought up short on this fact. A captive does not choose.

Yet, mysteriously, his work at the refining tub no longer seemed so deadly tedious a task as before. Now and again, to his surprise, he even caught himself gaining a distinct satisfaction in the doing of it.

Oddly, the wall between the huts had also changed somewhat. For, now and again it was not friend so much as barrier. More and more he was captivated by the life going on on the other side of it. One time, listening to a spate of laughter, he was so drawn into it that he himself laughed aloud, as if he were in truth sitting with the family group. But he sobered at once.

Yet, sometimes he couldn't keep himself from wondering what it would be like to be living that charmed life on the other side of the wall, to be a member without question, his place assured not by any effort on his part but by right of birth. Right or wrong, that's how he looked upon Elek's place in the scheme of things.

Even the mistress, of all people, seemed to have changed—and for the better. True, she was still as loud and shrill as ever. But no longer did she seem quite so frightening as before.

And this in spite of what happened one day when the dog belonging to a neighbor who lived near the end of the lane somehow got into the master's yard. Before the animal was discovered he had tromped all over the raw tiles that were lying out in the open air to dry. At least a third were imprinted so deeply with the hound's big paws that they had to be discarded.

The master took this mishap as part of the hazards of his craft, for, it seemed, the same thing happened not infrequently, and often with the same dog as culprit.

But not the mistress. Not that one! What a hulla-baloo, what a hoohaw she raised over the length of the entire lane that day! The noisy affair lasted until a promise was extracted from the wearied neighbors to keep their hound tied up at all times.

At first Bern was shocked by the mistress' unseemly aggressiveness. But, on second thought, was she not only looking out for her family's interests—just as she had said of the Princess Olha? On thinking it over, Bern decided that, shrill or not, in a pinch she was a good one to have on one's side, for all her boldness— or, come to think, because of it. Evidently the master and Elek believed this, too, for the three of them had a merry time of it at supper that evening.

And then came that bright and sunny day when Bern was sent to the city with baskets of tiles all by himself. Even before the master came into the kiln hut that morning Bern knew what was afoot, for, through the wall he had heard the following exchange.

The master: ". . . in that case, I'll send Bern alone. Surely he knows the way by now."

The mistress, shocked: "Whatever are you thinking of, husband? Why, he'll run off—and then where'll you be?"

The master: "But he's only a burden, I thought I

once heard you say—another mouth to feed."

The mistress, laughing: "Akh, you! How you do love to tease!"

So right after breakfast Bern was sent off with a load of tiles. As he went out the gate, he felt that if it were not for the pair of heavy baskets weighting him down, purely out of elation he would take flight like a bird and go soaring into the blue of the sky.

As he went hurrying as fast as he could up Borich's Wagon Road, he scarcely noted what he saw along the way. Even while, later, he was passing through the market, he did not pause in his haste to reach the church, where all manner of far more interesting activity was going on. This time, he promised himself, he would linger as long as he dared and watch as much as he could of the work going forward. He would watch the tilers, for one.

But, when he arrived breathless in the church, he saw at a glance that the tilers were not there that day. Instead, on a scaffold that had been erected behind the altar he saw other men at work. Going closer, he stood watching.

They were painting on the wall with little brushes. And under their hands human figures in various attitudes, clothed in long, flowing garments elegantly draped, were appearing upon the wall. Now at last Bern saw that the black lines that he had noticed on the walls during his first visit were not scrawls after all, but guides for painting the figures. The men worked with such swiftness that Bern was dazzled watching them, not even aware that he still held the heavy baskets.

Suddenly a big paw clapped him on the shoulder,

almost felling him.

"Well, so it's you, my boy!" Zhdan's voice boomed in his ear.

Hastily setting down the baskets, Bern turned. Before he knew what was happening, Zhdan had reached out and snatched his beloved cap right off his head. "I meant to tell you the other day," he said. "Doff your cap when you enter here."

Then, seeing the distress on Bern's face, he said, handing it back, "Here, no one wants your precious cap."

Hastily, without a word, Bern took it and stuffed it into the bosom of his tunic.

Then, as if to make amends for his bluntness, Zhdan said, "Look about if you wish. Look all about." He waved a hand toward the galleries. "Go up there, too, if you like—see how it all looks from there. But first unload the tiles."

With that, he strode off toward the scaffold behind the altar.

Bern stood a moment, unbelieving. Here was fortune again this day!

Stooping, as quickly as he could he emptied the baskets and with due care stacked the tiles. That done, he stood and looked all about.

On almost every side were the small archways inviting him into chambers he could just glimpse from where he stood. Choosing one at random, he passed through and came out into a smaller chamber. And there he found that on its every side were more archways, beckoning into still farther chambers.

On and on, to his intense delight, the archways led him into chamber after chamber, until at last he was quite lost within that maze. And then, suddenly, stepping unsuspecting through still another archway, he found himself in the big central chamber again, but underneath the gallery on the opposite side from which he had started.

He stood with a surprised smile on his face. Immediately to his left a flight of narrow steps led to the gallery above. They, too, invited him, and he started to climb them. At the top, he paused, then tiptoed to the parapet edging the gallery. When he reached it and looked, he caught his breath. He had not dreamed it would be like this.

The view was a revelation. The design of the mosaic and tile floor in front of the altar, though still unfinished, drew his eye toward the altar as a place of dramatic importance. For the first time he saw that the master's tiles, pleasing as they were, were but fragments of a grand design. So this is what the Great Princess Olha would see when she gazed from this very spot!

For a long time then, Bern stood bewitched by the ikon painters at work on the scaffold. It seemed to him that their work was magic. From his lofty place even the sounds of their voices as they talked among themselves echoed and hovered in the air like an otherworldly music.

But even this was not the all of it that day. As Bern was turning away at last, for the first time he noticed a small wooden chest standing on the floor against the parapet, its lid open. He tiptoed up and looked into it.

It was a toolbox. He knelt and one by one began examining the tools. He recognized the hammer, the hatchet, the chisel—but here was a curious two-headed tool the like of which he had never seen. And here was another that looked like a large thick needle. And here was a long piece of string with a weight on the end of it.

The realization came to Bern: these must be the tools that had built this church. He stared at them, marveling that such small implements in a man's hand could rear such a grand edifice.

Now he could not help himself. On impulse, he picked up the hammer and stood with it, hefting it in his hand. It felt good in his hand. Belonged there.

And—he was a builder . . . like Zhdan . . .

An unspeakably heady dream . . . so bold as to be frightening . . . truly an impossible dream . . .

Only, someone would have to show him how.

There was a sound behind him. Hastily he put the hammer back into the box.

Kari came up to him. "Those are the master's tools," he remarked. "He doesn't like them touched."

"I know," Bern murmured. "I didn't mean—I was just . . ."

Kari smiled. "It's all right," he said.

That day, so as to make up for lost time, Bern ran all the long way home, swinging the empty baskets, weaving his way nimbly around all comers. Above all, he mustn't give the master any cause for rebuke now!

After that memorable day, as often as not Bern was sent to the city alone. Whenever he could, he stole a moment to look over more of the church. By now he was recognized by the craftsmen so that curious glances were no longer sent his way. Sometimes he met briefly with Zhdan or Kari and now and then the master builder even gave him a message to carry back to the master.

More and more Bern marveled whenever he watched the work of embellishing the church. He marveled at the work of the tilers, of the ikon painters, and of the unknown wood carvers who had carved the great screen before the altar.

But most of all he marveled at the work of the carpenters who with hatchet, hammer—no more than a dozen tools in all—had built the monumental church itself. If only he could have been on hand to watch them rearing this edifice to the sky!

Nevertheless, whenever he thought of that dream he'd dared to dream, he did his best to thrust it out of his thoughts as being utterly impossible and therefore foolish. But he began to look upon his part in the making of tile as important—of prime importance, one might even say. For, without clay of fine quality, all the master's skill would go for nothing.

Less and less often now did the master find need to chide him for stray pebbles. On one occasion when the master had tested the clay that Bern had pronounced ready, as if he understood something, he threw Bern a certain brief glance that spoke an unspoken comradeship between them. Bern remembered that glance for days. He no longer wondered so much at the strange intensity with which the master bent over his work.

One day the master let the kiln go cold, so that for the first time in many a night Bern was not stifling from the heat. For some time he lay with eyes wide awake, enjoying the new comfort and listening to the talk on the other side of the wall.

The mistress was speaking. "Here is willow week upon us. We must begin preparations for Great Day."

Willow week . . . Great Day . . . Now what could they be?

"There's the hut to whitewash," the mistress went on, "the stove to rebuild, the scrubbing and the washing—"

"The kiln hut to see to," the master interposed. "A deal of work, but with each at his appointed task, we'll soon have it done."

"And now we have Bern to help." That was Elek.

"Bern?" There was a doubt in the mistress' voice. "Surely you don't mean we are to allow him to put his hand to these tasks?"

"But whyever not, wife?"

"But why not, he says!" The mistress' voice rose. "Why not, indeed! Ought I have to remind you that these are no ordinary tasks, that no profane hand ought to be put to them?"

"But wife, when will you get it into your head that the boy's one of our own people?"

"So say you," the mistress retorted. "But I say once a Pechenih, always a—"

"But he's no Pechenih!" This time it was Elek who came to Bern's defense.

"Then why is he so timid among us?"

"But when has he shown that lately?" the master demanded to know.

"Well . . . not visibly perhaps," the mistress conceded. "But inside!"

At this waywardness, the master and Elek burst out laughing, and the mistress, as if amused by her own caprice, joined in.

Bern stared into the darkness, frowning. How had she seen inside him?

"The boy's under our roof," the master went on when they had all subsided, "and must be included in our observance of Great Day whether you will or no. If animals must be included, so certainly must he. Besides, he's become a good helper and so has earned a place."

That last seemed to convince the mistress. "Very well. As you say."

Yet, though Bern listened to every word, he heard no clue as to what manner of day was Great Day.

The next day—it was the Monday —the mistress herself brought Bern his bowl of porridge. Bern took it with his usual exaggerated show of gratitude. Turning away with a look of disgust on her face, she left at once.

As Bern was settling down in his corner with the bowl, Elek came in. Sitting down at the worktable, with the small mortar placed between his knees, he began pounding away at some enamel, his lips up-turned and almost smiling.

In his corner Bern was just taking up his first spoon-ful of porridge when on top of it he noticed three small bits of something that looked like grey fur. They lay in the center of the bowl so evenly spaced in a three pointed star as to suggest that they had been arranged.

Bern glanced up at Elek. Elek was working away, the half smile still on his face.

Bern touched one of the bits of fur with his spoon, then turned it over. He stared at it. Then he picked it up between his thumb and forefinger and held it up to the light.

His face cleared. It was a catkin from a willow branch.

He looked up at Elek and this time he spoke. "There are catkins in my porridge," he announced.

Without ceasing his pounding Elek glanced over at him, laughter in his eyes. "Of course," he said.

"Of course?"

"That's what I said: of course. This is the first day of willow week. Don't the Pechenihs observe willow week?"

Bern slowly shook his head.

Elek interrupted the pounding. "They don't?" There was immense surprise in his voice. "But how, then, do they welcome the new sun? Or don't they?"

Bern thought a moment. They did welcome the return of the sun. But—he did not want to think about it.

"Well, do they or don't they?" Elek repeated.

Bern looked down at the bowl. "Yes, they do," he murmured.

But, suddenly recalling the mistress' unfriendly remarks of the evening before, he pushed the catkins aside and began to eat, gingerly. (Heaven only knew what else might be in that bowl!) Just as he was spooning up the last of the porridge, the mistress came down the steps. Bern stood and placed the bowl on the table beside Elek.

The mistress picked it up. "But what is this!" she exclaimed. "You've left the catkins?" She looked at Bern in astonishment.

Just then the master came in. "Just look at this, husband! He's refused the catkins!"

"Truly?" There was surprise in the master's voice, too. "Then so much the worse for him!" He gave Bern a brief frown.

105

A little later, when Bern was alone with Elek again, that one said to him, "You have offended my mother." When Bern made no reply, Elek went on. "She thought to include you in our spring rites. There's magic in the willow, you know. It gives a person some of its own new vigor after the long dark winter. Everything's now awakening after the winter's long sleep —trees and plants and animals—all things in nature! And people, too, of course. For earth and all that's in it is one, so humankind is one with nature. And then, too, in a few days our grandsires will be returning from their paradise on a visit, to see how we live, whether decently or badly. So we have to—"

"Grandsires?" Bern interrupted.

"Our departed ones," Elek explained.

"Departed ones?" Bern repeated. "The dead, you mean?"

Elek let go the pestle with a clatter. "Okh!" he cried. "Don't speak of them as dead! That's unseemly! Our people do not die. Don't you know that?"

He paused as if to regain his calm, then went on. "They go to a place called paradise, where the sun shines always bright and warm, and birds sing and flowers grow and fruits ripen overnight. But a number of times a year they come back to visit us in their old homes. So all this week, you see, we make preparation to welcome not only the new sun but our grandsires as well. Everything and everyone must be in the best of order, that they may see how well we manage their old homes and how well we treat all that's in our care."

Elek paused and gazed at nothing for a moment. "Not that one ever sees them . . . But then," he turned and smiled at Bern, "not all that's in the world is visible!"

That day all work on tiles was abandoned. Instead, every last thing that was loose in both huts was turned out—tables, benches, tub, tile forms, the heavy sacks of clay—everything but the kiln itself and that, evidently, only because it was well fastened to walls and floor. All was laid out in the yard till it took on the look of a bazaar. Judging by the sounds that occasionally came from the neighboring yards, people up and down the potters' lane were at the very same business that day.

It was hard work and there was not much talk, so Bern could not discover the purpose of all this activity. Elek had spoken of good order. But this seemed like disorder—like a madness, no less.

Finally, when they had everything in complete disarray, the mistress handed Elek a pair of brushes and a big pot of something she called whitewash. Under Elek's tutelage, with the brush Bern helped to smear the whitewash all over the walls of the kiln hut. All the while they were thus at work, the mistress was evidently at the same task in the hut. And, as if this were not enough, the master was whitewashing even the outside of the kiln hut.

At last, his bewilderment impelled Bern to ask, "What are we doing this for?"

Elek paused and looked at him in surprise with those round blue eyes of his, his brush poised in midair. "But I told you—Great Day's coming," he replied.

And, as if that told all, he resumed his task with more vigor than before.

When, late in the morning, they had finished, Bern

was astonished at the difference their work had made in the kiln hut. He had not suspected that soot had darkened the walls so much. And out of doors, too, the huts looked as bright as if new built.

After a scanty dinner and a briefer than usual noon rest, they all returned to the spring cleaning. While Bern was at work smoothing a fresh layer of clay on the floor of the kiln hut, the same was being done in the dwelling. And in the yard the master and Elek were scrubbing the tables and benches clean with fine sand brought up from the river shore. Later, the mistress carried out every pot, bowl, and utensil she owned and with the fine sand proceeded to scrub and wash them as well, every last one.

Till the very last ray of the sun had sunk behind the bluff everyone that day was in a fever of activity. By nightfall, scrubbed and clean, everything had been put right back where it had been. In the kiln hut, as Bern was neatly replacing all the things that belonged on the work table, he continued to wonder at the day's useless activity. It was as if some sort of madness had seized the lot of them.

But they weren't the only ones. The entire potters' lane had evidently been seized with the same fever. Why, for all he knew, the entire city had been infected! It chilled one's very blood to think of it. And he the only sane one among them all.

That night Bern listened to a rather heated discussion of the incident of the catkins on the other side of the wall.

"I suppose," the mistress was saying, "that among the Pechenihs he learned no proper customs—just remember how firm I had to be in the matter of eating with a spoon. Very likely the Pechenihs do not even trouble to greet the returning sun at this season of the year, as we Kiyans do. Very likely they live out their brutish lives without any sort of reverence for the powers that prevail invisible among us. They're probably totally ignorant of how humankind must conduct itself toward the righteous Sun, the father of all, who blesses the earth and all that's in it with its light and its warmth. Imagine! Casts aside the catkins as if they were rubbish! No good will come of that, I can tell you!"

"Okh, be still, wife! Ever one and the same tune . . ."

There was silence then.

All the same, the next day—the Tuesday—when the activity began all over again, Bern was very much a part of it. That morning they all worked at starting the mistress' garden in a corner of the yard. While the master dug, Bern and Elek followed on his heels, turning the soil under with some manure. Behind them came the mistress, hoe in hand, breaking up the clods. Even the hens joined in. They came running to feast on the earthworms and grubs turned up.

When the garden soil had been turned and hoed and freed of the horse-radish and other weed roots, the mistress herself prepared to plant. She brought out seed onion and garlic, each plaited together by their leaves, and little cloth sacks of beans and peas and lentils and the seed of the poppy as well. Bern was curious to watch, for the Pechenihs never planted anything, but lived off sheep's meat and mare's milk.

Unfortunately, however, the master set him to a task in the kiln hut, where he was now repairing the kiln. Part of the clay lining of the upper compartment had loosened from the woven withes that formed its skeleton and the pieces of it had begun dropping onto the tiles, spoiling some of them. The withes themselves had become scorched. So while the master was busy spreading a new lining of clay, thick and even, on the inside, Bern and Elek were at the same task on the outside of it.

They did not finish until late afternoon, and when for a brief moment Bern stepped out of doors at last, he saw that the mistress had evidently already finished the planting. And not only that, but by now she had wet clothes that she had evidently washed in the trough draped all along the fence, on the shrubs, and the greening grass to dry in the sun. Bern shook his head in amazement.

That night, the wall yielded Bern only scant talk before silence fell. Yet for a long time he could hear someone moving softly about. He lay listening hard. The mistress perhaps? What was she about? He fell asleep wondering.

The next morning, along with the porridge Elek brought something else. "Look," he said, holding out his hand.

Without meaning to, Bern drew in his breath. On Elek's palm lay what seemed to be a large, oval jewel of several colors. He reached to touch it.

Elek drew his hand quickly away. "No, don't touch. Just look. It's one of the eggs my mother decorated last night. At this season everyone carries one about for a talisman, for—see?—it is covered with magic signs of all sorts. No one goes anywhere without one."

Bern wondered whether there would be one for

him. But, for fear of the probable answer, he did not ask. At any rate, when Elek left the kiln hut he took the beautiful talisman with him.

That day, the mistress was busy the livelong day with baking bread and pastries of a special kind. Bern knew that this was what she was about because whenever he had occasion to pass the open doorway of the hut he caught whiffs of the delicious smells wafting out.

In the afternoon Bern was sent to the citadel with a miscellaneous lot of tiles that had turned up during the cleaning of the kiln hut and belonged in St. Sofia church for the use of the tilers. When he reached the marketplace he was surprised to find it nearly empty. Most stalls were shut and the atmosphere was almost sleepy. For lack of patrons, some venders were busying themselves with needlessly rearranging their wares. And at the city gate, for once Bern walked through without being jostled by crowds.

He found the same lull within the city and in the very church itself. Not one artisan was at work.

As Bern was emptying the baskets, Kari the apprentice came forward. "As you see," he said, waving a hand, "all work has come to a halt. Everyone is at home helping with preparations for Easter—or, I suppose, for Great Day."

Bern looked up. "Easter?"

Kari smiled. "Why, yes. That is the holy day that we Christians celebrate—precisely on Great Day, it so happens."

Though Great Day itself, with its singing and gladness, its dancing and games and garlands of flowers, as Elek described it, would not come till the following

Sunday, everything had to be ready by dusk on the Thursday before. For that was the night when one's departed grandsires returned for a brief visit to their old homes. At the master's, even by the Wednesday night nearly everything was in readiness.

Even the cat had not escaped attention, but was treated to a tasty piece of fish for her dinner that day. "For," Elek explained, "she does her bit for our household, just like the rest of us . . ."

Weary, Bern lay in the dark, enjoying an unexpected contentment from the new orderliness all about him and dreamily going over all of the activities of the days just past. With a kind of happy anticipation he thought of the coming Great Day, and vague memories stirred in him, as if he had known it all before. And a curious feeling came over him of having arrived home.

On the other side of the wall Elek brought up a new topic. "In the morning," he said, "I'll be going with the rest of the lads to gather fuel for the balefire tomorrow night."

"I suppose," the mistress remarked, "that you'll have it in the same place as last? Near the stream down there in the swamp forest? By rights you ought to have it nearer the water, so that the flames, reflected in it, will double the light."

"That's true," the master put in. "So my mother always used to say, that the balefires of Great Day season ought always to be near water. Double the light and so double the honor paid the Sun—light the way twice-bright for our returning kin. So my mother always used to say."

Then Elek said something that made Bern sit up.

"Should I take Bern along to help gather the fuel or not?" he asked.

Bern held his breath, waiting for the answer. If there was one thing he knew about it was fires. He had spent almost every evening of his life on the edges of the group around the campfire on the steppe. And it had always been his task to find fuel—no easy one in that treeless land!

"But do you forget," the mistress was saying, "how he refused the catkins? Would you have him blight so sacred a thing as the balefire? Okh, he's sure to bring ill fortune down upon this house!"

"Hush, wife! Do you forget yourself? At this season one must think only good and speak only good."

A pause. Were they exchanging glances?

"Great Day among all days in the year ought to be the most joyous," the master continued.

Another pause.

"Take him along, my son," the master said at last. "Just see to it that you gather only the best of fuel. Let this be the best of all balefires! For last year, it seems to me, the tanners had a better one than we in potters' lane."

From the mistress came not a murmur.

 Right after noon rest the next day the youths of the lane, led by Yan, set forth to collect fuel for the coming night's balefire. And Bern was allowed to join them. Though he was happier than he dared show to be thus included in the band of youths ranging the lane, he took care always to tag along at the rear. For, it would not do to push oneself forward too much.

Up and down the lane they trooped, setting the dogs to barking, as they collected trough and tub, lid and paddle, mortar and wagon shaft, cask and cart wheel, bucket and bin—and any other wooden thing that fell to their hands. They spurned only logs felled by the ax, windfall timber, and driftwood from the river shore as unfit for the sacred fire.

When, at last, they got to the master's gate, which was a stout plank of oak, to Bern's astonishment they began ripping it from its hinges. To his further astonishment, the master was standing within sight and sound, yet did not try to stop them.

"Well, wife," he called into the hut, "this year they're making off with our gate!"

The mistress stepped to the doorway and glanced out. "So they are," she cried cheerfully. "We don't grudge it. So much the brighter our greeting to our returning grandsires!"

By late afternoon, the youths of the potters' lane had collected an immense pile of fuel and stacked it all at the bottom of the lane. Then they dispersed briefly to their huts, to meet again at dusk.

When, at dusk, Bern stood in the doorway of the master's dwelling waiting for Elek to set out for the forest, he had one of his infrequent glimpses into the heart of the master's world. He watched as the master lit the trio of candles that he and the mistress together had made that morning and that was to burn all the night. Its light filled the hut with a gentleness and warmth, transforming all in it. Miraculously, even the mistress' features were softened, and an unwonted smile lit her eyes. The fragrance of the good food, cooked and waiting for Great Day's feasting, lingered in the air.

At last, the two boys set forth. Silently Bern followed Elek out through the gateway and down to the bottom of the lane, where most of the others were already waiting beside the pile of fuel. Scarcely a word was spoken.

Bern stood gazing down upon the river far below. At intervals along the shore, as far as he could see, the sky was already reflecting the red of balefires. Even across the river, above the forest that grew there, he could see the glow of still others, probably lit by fishermen who had rowed across.

In accord with custom, so Elek had told him, no one would sleep this night of the great return of the grandsires from that paradise of theirs, that distant realm that lies beyond thrice-nine kingdoms. Now by dusk in every hut and in almost every palace (understood, not in those inhabited by Christians), the sacred trio of beeswax candles had been lit to burn the long night through and light the way for the returning spirits.

Truly, this night would be aflame with welcome!

At last, when all the youths of the potters' lane had gathered, at a signal from Yan, each picked up some piece from the heap of fuel. The heavier pieces, such as the troughs and wheels and wagon shafts, were hoisted by two together and even more. Bern helped Elek lift a heavy cart wheel between them. None was going empty handed to the balefire.

At length, with Yan in the lead, they set forth for the swamp forest, where they would build their balefire. But instead of going by way of Borich's Wagon Road, Yan led them scrambling down the steep bare slope of the bluff, straight for the forest at the bottom.

Now, only a few steps ahead, there it stood, waiting to receive them. Bern could not remember ever having been in a forest before. Without meaning to, he shuddered with a thrill of dread.

But, keeping a firm hold on his fear, he stepped in among the pines. Dense tufts of sedge grass grew in hummocks between them, making islands in the mire. Led by Yan, they leaped from hummock to hummock, winding their way through the gloom deeper and deeper into the forest.

The pines were tall, not large in girth, but with arms spread wide, and the distance between them allowed vistas into the depths of the forest. Far down those vistas something seemed to glow and the air all about quivered as if with echoes dying. Even the ground, wherever it was solid enough to step on, seemed to quiver under one's tread. The brown smell of decaying plants hung thick in the air. But Bern found it not at all unpleasant.

As often as not, Bern missed the hummock he and Elek were leaping for and landed in the mire, and the others the same. But no one laughed. In spite of the heavy cart wheel that Bern was helping to carry, he moved almost lightly, gazing with a curious pleasure down the vistas that opened to him with every step.

They were veering sharply to the left now, and in a few moments Bern heard the voice of a stream. A few moments more and they reached it, a rather sizable one flowing through the forest toward the Dnipro. It was nearly dark by now. But at a distance, in the direction of the Dnipro, a big red blaze could be seen. Some Kiyans, evidently, had lit a huge balefire.

One by one as the youths came up they dropped their loads onto the growing pile of firewood. Several had already begun gathering dry twigs and heaping them for kindling. Others, choosing some of the smaller pieces from the pile of firewood, began laying the fire.

Yan knelt, a sharp-pointed stick and a small slab of wood in his hand. Putting the little slab on the ground, he lay bits of fluffed-up tow over it. Then placing the point of the sharp stick on the slab, he began twirling it between his palms and blowing on the tow to get the living fire. Four of the youths stood with faggots ready. Silently, the rest encircled them.

"There," some one said softly as a wisp of smoke began curling upward from the bits of tow.

In a few moments the faggots had been lit and the four youths, one to a side, took their stand around the wood laid for the balefire. There came a moment's pause while they composed themselves for the ritual.

Then, stepping forward as one, they laid their flaming faggots to the wood, slowly chanting in unison:

"Light! Give light, O righteous Sun,
Round and round dear mother earth!
Flame, enflame the goddess Spring—
Go! Begone, all evil things!"

Soon the wood was flaming tall, roaring and crackling, and sparks danced zigzag to the sky. A wind sprang up. The stream, ablaze with the reflected flames, flowed fire-red.

Now the youths sat down around the fire, and Bern, waiting till they had done so, took a place on the edge of the circle. He had not sat by a fire since his days among the Pechenihs.

Solemnly, and even anxiously, they all sat staring into it, their faces transmuted by the flickering shadows cast by the flames. At length even the trees that ringed the clearing were transformed. Whether it was the shadows cast by the flames, or something else, they now loomed giant-tall. Just beyond lay the pitch black night, encircling the big red eye of the balefire flaming within the ring of youths within the ring of trees. And all the world beyond had vanished.

Bern sat staring fixedly into the fire. And after a long while there came to him the certain knowledge that he was gazing into the distant, mysterious beginning of things. Then he became one with the flames, so that for a long time he was unable to glance away. But at last, when a spark broke from the flames, he followed it till it danced out of sight into the sky.

He glanced around then at the circle of youths. He was one with them, too. One with Kiyans. "We Kiyans"—that phrase that was such a favorite of the mistress—began murmuring in his head.

He ducked his chin and smiled to himself, pleased but—truth to tell—half-frightened. Wasn't his unusual contentment merely the result of his taking part in the master's sacred rites? Oughtn't he be wary? For experience, if it had taught him anything, had taught him that a master might one moment seem all friendliness, all welcome, might even grant him a glimpse into his warm, bright world, and the next moment, by some word or act or gesture, shove him right out.

No one talked. But from the depths of the night all around them came mysterious whisperings, rustling sounds, and now and again the sharp crack of a twig broken. From time to time Yan's or some other's voice softly sang out, "Mend the fire!"

Then several sprang up, ran to the woodpile, and dragged out a table, a bench, or some other perfectly good piece of household furnishing. Carrying it to the edge of the balefire, with a mighty swing and a "bai—i—RUP!" they heaved it square into the flames. As it crashed, sending plumes of sparks into the sky, a long drawn out "Ah—h—h!" came from the circle of youths.

On each such occasion Bern considered jumping up to help with mending the fire. But each time, on second thought, regretfully, he decided against it. Better not to risk rebuff . . .

After a while, as the night wore on, here and there voices began quiet conversation. Last year's fire was recalled, or the one before that. But now and then a laugh broke out. Instantly it was stifled with low, indignant outcries.

"Here, you two!"

"Are you beside the cattle or what?"

"The most sacred time of the year and you behave

like clowns in the bazaar?"

Thus throughout the night the youths sat, hugging their knees, their faces reddened by the roasting heat. Now and again someone rose to stretch legs and arms. A few of the younger ones began to nod until prodded awake.

At long last came a certain stirring of the wind, no more than a light soughing. Next, someone wordlessly pointed through the trees toward the Dnipro. Sure enough, in that direction the night was paling. Several of the boys now slowly got to their feet.

Elek came and at last sat down beside Bern. "Here you are," he said, giving Bern one of his broad, open smiles, "among all these strangers!"

Bern turned and stared at him, astounded. What could possibly have prompted Elek to utter such a thought? Here was Bern, for the first time feeling himself one with Kiyans, and this one came to tell him that in truth he was not.

Disheartened, Bern turned away and stared unseeing into the balefire. But its spell was shattered.

Just then, from somewhere out in the forest came shouts. All jumped to their feet. In the next moment two men came bounding in among them. "Leave all this!" one shouted.

Yan came forward. "Leave it? Why so, friend?"

"They're hard on their way! That's why! If you value your life—"

"But who? Who?" voices asked.

"Those to the south that harry our merchants— Pechenihs!"

"They're on their way! Thousands!" the other man cried. "We can't stop now—have to alarm . . ."

In the next instant both men were gone.

 In those days, so near to the end of her life, the Princess Olha, together with her three young grandsons, kept to her favorite residence, there on Castle Hill. Usually she ventured forth only on matters of state that required her presence elsewhere and on great holy days of her Christian belief, which she sometimes celebrated in St. Iliia's, the church in the swamp forest.

It so happened that that year, as if by design, such a holy day, the movable feast named Easter, was to fall upon the very same day as Great Day. During the days just before Easter, the Princess went early every morning to church. So that during the early hours of that Friday, while balefires were blazing bright all roundabout Kiev, the old Princess was in St. Iliia's church.

And there, that dawn, word was brought her that a great horde of nomads was hard on its way toward Kiev and that soon the city would be under attack.

At this sudden threat of danger the Princess sum-moned up the strength, from somewhere within her frail old person, to take brief command. She sent at once for her grandsons to be conducted to the safety of the castle within the walls of the city. Then she dispatched four messengers, two by water and two by land, to distant Volharia, where with his forces her son Sviatoslau was hanging his victorious shield upon city after city of that kingdom. The message was short: Come home—rescue your city and your sons.

She did this in spite of her stated opinion that the Pechenihs had been sent to attack Kiev-land (by no other than the crafty Greeks) precisely to divert Sviatoslau from his victories. She further gave it as her sorrowful opinion that the pagan balefires of her people had lit the way for the invader.

As ill luck would have it, the commander Pretich, with most of the city's garrison, which in any case numbered no more than a few hundred men, was absent from the city. For, to replenish the princely larder, they had crossed the Dnipro the day before to follow the chase for a day or two in the forest preserve just opposite the city. They were so deep in the forest by then that they could not be found at once. The Princess therefore gave command that the guard upon the city wall be strengthened from among Kiyans themselves.

Next, she gave command that all Kiyans who dwelt outside the city wall be let inside, the bridge then drawn and the gate shut that none might leave or enter. Every Kiyan must keep weapon ready to hand. Those without weapon were to apply at the princely storehouse in the citadel. Thus secured behind their wall, Kiyans might outwait the nomad invaders and so weather the danger.

Although rarely in all its history of hundreds of years had the city been under attack—and certainly not within the memory of any living Kiyan—prompted by natural impulse, they knew what to do. Those who lived outside the wall quickly packed food and, with what weapons they owned, made all haste for the city. Early that morning Borich's Wagon Road was thronged. For outside the wall in those days lived not only the potters, but also the blacksmiths, the tanners, the fishermen, the keepers of the princely forests, the princely huntsmen, and a scattering of others.

When Bern and Elek, along with the other boys of the lane, reached home that early dawn, their chests heaving from their race through the forest and up the side of the bluff, they found the master already pouring the millet out of the big heavy storage jars into baskets. Seeing the two boys come dashing into the yard, he said, "Good, here you are at last! You, Elek, go fetch the other jar of millet out of the house and also bring out the hatchet. And you," he said to Bern, "go into the kiln hut and bring out all the enamels in a basket."

Bern flew to do the master's bidding. But in the hut he first hastily plucked up his sheepskin and cap and put them on. Then he thrust several chunks of bread he had been saving into the bosom of his tunic. As he stepped out with the basket of enamels there was a call from the gateway. "Coming, neighbor? Better not to linger!"

"Coming! Coming!" the mistress cried as she struggled out of the hut carrying a large basket filled with the big new-baked loaves of bread. Bern noticed that in among the loaves she had tucked the talisman-eggs she had decorated. "Ready, husband?" she said.

The master was fastening to his belt the hatchet that Elek had brought out. "Ready," he said.

As if noticing Bern for the first time, the mistress said, pointing to one of the baskets filled with millet, "You carry that, too."

Out in the lane they joined a little stream of people as burdened as they. In silence they trudged along. Borich's Wagon Road, when they reached it at last, was a broad stream of people all climbing toward the city, which brooded over them in the dawn's grey light. Hardly a word was spoken. Most carried baskets of grain and other food and whatever tools of their crafts were both valuable and portable. Some were even carrying cages of live poultry. Almost every man had a hatchet fastened to his belt.

As they were turning onto the road, Bern glanced southward. They would be coming from that direction. He strove to keep his face bland, strove to quiet the eagerness that, against his most profound desire, had sprung up in him.

Suddenly, a strident voice behind them shouted, "Make way! Make way for the Princess!"

Along with the others Bern crowded to the side of the road and watched as the small procession approached and passed. Mounted guardsmen came before and after the Princess' chair. To Bern's surprise, its curtains were open and in its shadows he caught a glimpse of a figure that seemed mounded with furs.

"Akh, poor old soul!" breathed a voice beside him. "Abandoned by her son . . ."

"And aren't we all? What's to become of us, I ask you, with the Prince gone and no army ready at hand? How defend ourselves?"

"She'll find some way, never fear. She's a shrewd one!"

"Yes, just remember how cleverly she dealt with the Derevlians—and now how nicely they eat out of her hand!"

"But I can't help wondering whether that new belief of hers has not brought this down upon us."

"So do I wonder, neighbor. And just what luck has that God of hers brought her? Just tell me that!"

As soon as the Princess and her guardsmen had passed, the crowd closed in behind and silently continued the climb.

By the time they reached the gates of the city the sky had already turned light blue. Here they were forced to come to a halt at last, for the gates were far too narrow for the throng that had already packed up in front of them. The crush became so great that at times the crowd hovered on the very edge of panic. From the towers on either side of the gate the harsh Norse voices prodded it on. "Move! Move!" they roared.

At last, somehow—no telling how—the master, Bern, and the others managed to squeeze through the gateway and into the safety behind the walls. Without even pausing for breath, the master led them the way to a little lane on their left that followed along the inner side of the city wall. When they reached a certain dwelling some distance along it, they paused at the gate in front of it. The mistress nodded toward Bern. "And so what about him?" she asked.

Frowning, the master made no reply, but led the way through the gate. No sooner had they stepped inside the yard than a man and a woman came hurrying out toward them. "Akh, my dears, thank goodness you've come!" the woman cried. "Come in—be so kind!"

"Do!" the man said, bowing and smiling. "Come in and welcome, kinsmen! Our house is yours!"

He led the way toward the hut. Bern, uncertain whether he was to follow, hesitated for an instant, and then fell in with the rest. The hostess glanced at Bern's cap and said, "And this is the lad you told me of that day we met in the market? The one from the Pechenihs?"

"The same," the master replied. "Perhaps you'll find room for him somewhere in your yard . . ."

Smiling, the woman glanced at Bern's cap again. "Why, as for that . . ." her voice trailed off.

Inside the hut Bern put down his burden with the others on the table. Then, a kind of confusion came over him. He hesitated a moment, then stepped back outside. And he knew as he did so that he was making a mistake of some kind, perhaps a fatal one. Not knowing what next to do, he hung about the doorway.

Presently, from the hut came a heated exchange.

"But might he not spy upon us?" That was the kinswoman speaking.

"True!" her husband put in. "And thus deliver us over to the Pechenihs so much the more quickly!"

"But are you mad, kinsman?" the master cried, anger in his voice. "How's he to do that? Besides, he's—"

"Well, husband," the mistress now broke in, "since he's not welcome here—there's nothing for it but to send him on his way. Even at that, he might be better off free to fend for himself. I've felt that all along, as well you know."

"Good!" quickly the other woman put in. "But here

—take this. At least send him off with a loaf of bread."
There was an angry exclamation from the master.

"Well, husband," the mistress cried, "I've tried to tell you all along that no good would come of it!"

Bern, listening, stood a moment, stunned. Then, his knees shaking, he made for the gate. Just as he shut it, behind it he heard the master's voice. "Why, he's gone! He's fled! Now just see what you've done!"

The sky overhead had already turned to bright blue when Bern found himself back at the city gate. The crowds coming through were not so thick as before. As he stood watching, impassive and hesitating, the thought came to him that of all those hundreds, he alone knew their foe, and he knew him as intimately as the palm of his own hand. As a matter of fact, there were some Kiyans who till that day had scarce heard even the name of Pechenih.

Bern stood watching the last of a few stragglers come hurrying through, his thoughts so numbed that he could not make up his mind. At last he saw that the gate was being lowered, ever so slowly.

It was deciding his fate. And still he could not move, but stood as if rooted to the spot, watching in fascination as slowly it moved down, down, down until at last, with a great thud, it met the pavement.

He turned away. His fate had been decided for him, and there was an odd comfort in that.

In Kiev that night no one slept. No one had even the thought of sleeping, as tensely the city waited for the appearance of the Pechenihs. Many, unable to contain themselves in their huts, thronged the streets, ears alert for unusual sounds.

Wandering restlessly, even strangers stopped and

struck up conversations with one another, as if in acknowledgement of an old kinship, as if their old tribal feelings had somehow magically surfaced from the depths of their souls.

Bern, too, wandered.

And as the night wore on he felt himself partly recovering from the death blow. Yet, though he walked about right enough, he felt his spirit to be in total collapse, with no hope of ever again traversing the long way it had come.

He found himself recalling a boy among the Pechenihs who had had a little fox that he kept in a cage woven of reeds. He had raised it from infancy, feeding it with a rag soaked in mare's milk, which it sucked. One time, when it was grown, by mistake the boy left its cage open. When the animal discovered the open door, it retreated to a corner of its cage and lay there trembling and cowering until someone noticed the door open and latched it again.

At the time, Bern marveled that not once had the little animal ventured even its muzzle through the open door. For a long time afterwards, whenever he thought about it, without meaning to, he shuddered.

But now he understood the little fox.

He, too, was terrified of freedom.

**15** Not until dawn of the next day was the first of the horde of Pechenihs sighted from the city. But long before that their approach was heard. On the soft morning air came a sound, at first only an undertone, that made every Kiyan lift his head and listen. Louder and gradually louder it grew, until it became the rattle of supply wagons, the neighing of numberless horses and the shouts of herdsmen driving them on. Soon the sound could be heard encroaching on every side, as nomads by the thousands filled the wooded vales to the north and south and west and the harbor quarter below.

After that, the guards on the wall had not long to wait before getting a closer look at some of the Pechenihs. They appeared suddenly—not more than a score of mounted men—over the brow of the bluff on the far edge of the field of barrows to the west of the city. Halting just on the brow, they stood gazing across that field at the city silhouetted by the rising sun. Then, urging their horses, at an easy trot they approached.

The small force of guards on the battlement, reinforced by ordinary Kiyans, stood tense, bow stretched and boulder poised on the edge. Silently they watched

the steady advance of the band of nomads, well lit by the sun.

They noted first their distinctive caps. With bow and quiver over the shoulder, every Pechenih but one was mounted on the short, shaggy, big-headed steppe pony, the tarpan. A single figure at their fore was mounted on what looked to be an Arabian horse. This one, resplendent in a mail shirt that rippled and glistened in the sun—stolen, without doubt—was taken to be their chief.

At last the band of Pechenihs came within bow-shot. Halting in front of the city gates, covered now by the bridge drawn up against it, they peered up at the battlement.

Suddenly, from the battlement the guards let fly a cloud of arrows. The nomads wheeled, went careering back across the field of barrows, and disappeared over the brow of the bluff.

Those on the wall took a deep breath, then braced themselves for the assault that was coming. For without doubt the invaders meant to storm the city and gain entry without delay.

And sure enough, in a short while horsemen again appeared over the brow, this time bearing flaming torches. They halted near the edge as wave after wave came up behind them. When the forces had grown near to a thousand, at a signal, yowling like the catamount in the forest, hardly slowed by the barrows in their path, they came galloping headlong across the field for the city.

Reaching the ditch in front of the wall, the first waves, pushed on by those behind them, plunged into it. Then, mercilessly urging their horses, they tried to climb the steep slope of the earthwork as if they meant to reach the top of it. But the horses fell screaming and rolling back into the ditch, dragging their riders with them. Arrows and stones rained down on them from the battlement.

Those who had managed to stop short of the ditch hurled the flaming torches up at the battlement. Most fell short, rolling down the clay slope to the bottom of the wall, where they were a long time burning themselves out. Those few that reached their mark were hurled straight back at the foe. Not one fell within the city or on the battlement roof.

At length, when the nomads saw that their firebrands had failed to set the battlement aflame, they stood ranged just out of bowshot, hurling insults instead. In this, too, the guards and Kiyans atop the wall gave back as good as they got.

Finally, however, tired of the useless sport, the Pechenihs began turning away. And then those on the wall had to watch helpless as the nomads put the torch to one after another of the huts outside the wall and burned them down, every one. The stalls of the Old Women's Market had of course long before been toppled and trampled to pieces. One band forced the princely castle nearby and stripped it clean of every treasure, judging by what they were seen to carry away. Fortunately, the great hall of that palace was of stone, so it escaped the flames.

At long length the Pechenihs began retreating from the field of barrows, disappearing over the brow and down off the bluff.

Silence fell.

Kiyans in their huts lifted their heads, puzzled and

fearful of what the silence might mean.

That same morning, the day before Great Day, those guarding the wall on the opposite side of the city, that overlooking the river, watched an incident that disheartened them all. A number of ferryboats loaded with men was seen to take off from the opposite shore and make for the city. As they drew near, those on the wall knew them to be the party that had gone on the chase with commander Pretich two days before. Evidently they had only just emerged from the forest, and no doubt they had been told the news of the city's plight by the fishermen stranded on the opposite shore.

Helplessly, unable to warn them of the danger that awaited, those on the wall watched the approach of the boats. As soon as they got within bowshot of the shore, Pechenihs sent swarms of arrows straight into the boats. Hastily the oarsmen turned the boats about and beat retreat as the men atop the wall gloomily watched them go. Though the force with Pretich was not great, it would have almost doubled the number of guardsmen within the city.

By this time the nomads had overrun the harbor quarter and the other settlements outside the city wall, putting the torch to everything in their path. The new ships riding at anchor on the river, the huts of the tanners, of the potters—all went up in flames. The princely castle on its hill above the potters' lane was pillaged, then burned.

Those sitting tense in the huts behind the city wall could see none of this. But they smelled the dust raised by the foe's immense herds, heard the yells, heard the neighing, smelled the smoke of hut and palace going up in flames.

Late that afternoon, so those manning the walls reported, Pechenihs reappeared on the field of barrows. But this time they pitched camp. Judging by the quality and cut of the most prominent tent, the camp was that of their chief. There, brazen as you please, he settled in as if for a long stay.

That night was the eve of Great Day, for Kiyans the most sacred time of the year. But no balefires burned to greet the righteous Sun. Instead, the city of Kiev was ringed round with the numberless campfires of the invader, their ruddy glow profaning the gentle night's sky overhead.

On the steppe in autumn the wind sweeps the dying land, uprooting the dried grass and neatly forming enormous balls of it into tumbling weeds. It will not permit them to come to rest anywhere for long, but amuses itself with rolling them long distances hither and yon across the endless land.

Driven by his search for he scarcely knew what, Bern wandered the city as rootless as the tumbling weeds he used to chase across the steppe. Even though from many parts of the city he caught glimpses of the cluster of domes that had once cast such a spell over him, deliberately he now shunned the church. Even thinking about it caused him a stab of pain.

For the first few nights of his total freedom Bern found shelter against a wattle fence in some one of the narrow lanes of the city. The chunks of bread he carried in the bosom of his tunic were sustaining him, and if he were careful they would last him fully a week. For drink he had only to step up to any well and help himself.

One night, thinking to better himself, he took refuge in the nook between two of the stalls set into the inner wall just to the right of the city gate. Here, out of sight of passersby, he found greater contentment

136

than in the open against a fence.

Unfortunately, however, his contentment was so great that the next morning he overslept and so was discovered by one of the stallkeepers. Spying him huddled there upon a bit of straw, she gave a startled little cry.

Bern woke. Seeing the woman standing there, slowly he got to his feet. But then, feeling of his head and noting that his cap had come off while he slept, he searched for it in the straw, found it, and put it on.

Bern was completely unprepared for what followed. The moment the woman saw the cap she clapped her hand to her mouth. Then she screamed. Several people came running. The woman pointed at Bern. "Pechenih!" she managed to gasp.

Bern stood dumbfounded.

By now a small crowd had gathered, surrounding him. "What is it? What's happened?" voices said.

"I don't know. I was just passing by . . ."

"Some youngster, I think . . ."

"Who? What did he do?"

And then someone repeated the word "Pechenih." The word was tossed about by the crowd and with each utterance the crowd pressed more and more closely upon Bern. He stood, shoulders hunched to receive what blows would come his way. But his passiveness did not mollify the crowd. Hands reached out and began plucking at his clothing. Bern's eyes darted about, but he saw only hostile faces on every side.

Suddenly, from the back of the crowd came a voice, and it was a familiar one. "What's this?" it asked.

"Some Pechenih has somehow wormed his way in," someone answered.

"Pechenih!"

The crowd parted and Zhdan the master builder came pushing his way through to the center of it. He gave one look at Bern and burst into a guffaw. "This is your Pechenih?" he cried. "Why, he's no Pechenih, you fools!"

"But look at his cap!"

"Yes!" cried another voice, "we all know that cap by now—only too well!"

"Cap or no cap," Zhdan retorted. "This is that youngster that the tilemaker in the potters' lane keeps."

A sigh went up from the crowd. Then rapidly it melted away until in a moment or two only Zhdan and Bern stood facing each other. Zhdan gave him an angry look. "Why don't you throw that headgear away?" he said.

And without waiting for an answer, he strode off in the direction of the church.

Slowly Bern raised his hand to his head and pulled off the cap. For a long moment he stood turning it over and over. Then he thrust it into his bosom along with the bread. Certainly he would not throw it away!

When, a day or two after that incident, Bern had eaten the last of his bread, he decided to go back to the stalls along the wall. Perhaps there he would find some scrap dropped to the ground.

When he reached there, luck came to his side almost at once. As he was slowly passing by a stall where poultry was still being sold—as if the stallkeeper could not get it into his head that ordinary times had vanished—he stopped to look at the cage of live chickens on the ground beside the stall. They were poking their heads out between the withes.

The stallkeeper had just taken one of the hens out of the cage and was holding it up for a patron's inspection. Evidently he had neglected to fasten the door of the cage, for in a moment Bern noticed a hen squeezing its way out. The stallkeeper also saw. But as he stooped to seize the hen, it darted off.

Seeing his chance at once, Bern went chasing hither-thither after it. At length he caught it and brought it back to the stallkeeper.

Somewhat surprised, the stallkeeper gave him a small portion of a loaf that was to be his own dinner. Bern took it with his usual great show of gratitude. The stallkeeper frowned. "No need to fawn quite so much, boy," he said.

Bern made no reply, but broke the bread in two, thrust one half into his bosom for safekeeping, and wolfed the other. The stallkeeper looked away.

With that good turn of events, the next day again Bern hung about that same stall, watching his chance. This time he appointed himself doorkeeper of the cage. He flew to open and close it for the stallkeeper whenever he waited on a patron. Several times that day he swept up around the stall with a besom he found behind it. Again that day the stallkeeper gave him a chunk of bread.

But the third day Bern's scheme fell to the ground. This time, no sooner did the stallkeeper notice Bern hanging about, obviously awaiting a chance to do him some unasked for and in truth unneeded service, than he spoke. "Now be off with you, boy. Find yourself a master elsewhere. I have too many mouths to feed as it is."

Bern went.

Having failed in that attempt to get himself a new master, all that day he wandered hungry about the city, totally without courage after the morning's rebuff. All the while, he puzzled over the difficulty of finding a master among the people of Kiev. Evidently the mistress was not alone among Kiyans in shunning one who sought servitude.

And yet, on further thought, perhaps it was not so much a master he sought as a place in the scheme of things, a place that was without any question his very own, a place so assured to him that he could never be turned out of it by anyone, under any circumstances. Elek had such a place. Yan had such a place. Kari . . .

The next day, with some such vague thought bumbling about in his head, Bern found himself in front of the church at last. For a long while he stood uncertain, staring at the door. It was slightly ajar. Mildly surprised at this, he continued to stand there. At last, however, he tiptoed up to it and, first glancing swiftly behind him, slipped inside.

In the church no sound of voices, no sound of artisans at work—only that vibrant stillness of a place once peopled and now empty. Bern stood a moment, trying to still the loud thumping of his heart. At last he tiptoed to the very center of the church and stood there, gazing up at the wondrously carved screen. Here was the place where he had dreamed that dream so grand, so brief, so foolish. So dead. He shivered. In spite of the brilliant sunshine out of doors, there was a peculiar chill in the church.

As he stood there, too late he heard someone behind him. He turned and saw Zhdan the master builder coming toward him. As he drew near, Bern saw how

140

altered was the builder's face, the eyes sunken and stricken, but oddly soft and glittering. His beard had grown, but even so, beneath it one could see that the cheeks were cavernous. Bern touched his hand to his cheek, wondering whether he, too, had altered.

As if he thought guilt was apparent on him, he made explanation. "I only wanted to look," he said.

"Ah, yes," the master builder replied. And his voice was altered as well. "I, too, love this place which is our handiwork."

From beneath his brows Bern stole a glance at him. He would not have put it that way. But, on second thought, there was some truth there. He did love this place, and precisely because of the handiwork that had made it.

Zhdan was speaking again. "Did you know that my apprentice Kari is lost?"

Bern looked up.

"Yes. Lost. A Pechenih arrow in the throat as he defended the wall with the guards . . . And all that I taught him—gone with him."

Without another word the master builder turned and slowly made his way toward the shadows beneath the gallery.

Out of doors again, Bern stood for a long time in the portico of the church, staring moodily toward the center of the city. Though every hut was packed to bursting, scarcely a soul was abroad. As he stood there, he heard a sound behind him—Zhdan, probably, coming out. Bern darted off the portico and ducked around the corner of the church.

He did not stop till he had reached the back of it. There, all the way from the church to the city wall a stone's throw distant, the stalks of last year's weeds stood tall. Idly, Bern followed along the church wall, and when he came to a niche in it formed by two portions of the structure meeting at an odd angle, he stopped and sat down. Leaning his back against the church wall, he looked about. Overhead, the broad eave roofed the niche. In front, the tall weeds secluded it.

Slowly, a smile grew on Bern's face. He sat and hugged his knees in very delight. It was perfect. He had found a home.

No one came to that part of the churchyard where Bern's home was. Yet, since it was his home, he had to take care to guard it against intruders. He was careful, for example, not to beat a path through the weeds, that no one be led to his niche. Always he made sure that no one saw him going around toward the back of the church.

Whenever he returned to his niche he found it undisturbed. That in itself gave him comfort, for it meant that it was in truth a home, a refuge. He had gathered weeds for a bed and always brought home to eat whatever food he had been able to find in the city instead of bolting it on the spot.

When he sat in his house, safe from everything and everyone, he felt the same coziness he knew from his life among the Pechenihs, when in winter, while the wind swept ceaselessly across the vasty steppe, they sat in the warm tent where the smells of horse, dog, sheep, cattle, and human mingled with those of wet wool and sheepskins and of cooking food. Only the human voices were missing.

Every day, usually in the morning, Bern left his niche to forage in the city. Though the sky over Kiev was never so blue, beneath that blue sky the besieged city was dying. One by one people had been giving up their accustomed activities as senseless in the circumstances and requiring more of strength than they had left. Among the stalls there was nothing to be bought now but useless gewgaws that had utterly lost their fascination. The grain bins were empty.

The streets, once thronged with people day and night, were almost deserted, and overhung with an eeriness that prompted Bern almost to tiptoe his way about. Gradually, the voices of the once energetic, thriving city—the hubble-bubble of the marketplace, the clop-clop of horses' hoofs, the rattle of wagon wheels and the shouts of wagoners, the cries of children at play—were stilled, every one. But the rooks, more raucous than ever on the still air, cawed from the treetops the livelong days.

Shut up behind their city wall, most Kiyans were spared the sight of the horde of nomads surrounding their city on every side. But the sounds and smells and other signs of the horde were with them day and night.

At night the skies over the city were lurid with the blaze of their campfires, and the air made ghastly with their shouting and yowling as night after night they danced and brawled. Their great herds of horses, trampling the tender new growth in the vales as they grazed, soon made dust of them. The herds were so great, confined to such a small area, that often their stink wafted across the city like an invisible poison.

Every day bands of mounted Pechenihs probed the city's defenses for weaknesses. While others waited in readiness a short distance away, they sent arrows and firebrands up into the battlements. When they received answering arrows and the return of their firebrands, they trotted back to camp, seemingly content enough. Obviously they were relying upon their own patience or the Kiyans' growing hunger to open the city gates for them. With scarcely effort on their part, one or the other would bring them victory.

And, as a matter of fact, within two weeks after the Kiyans had shut themselves within their wall, hunger was already pinching them, rich and poor alike, for even in ordinary times the spring season is the hungry season. The pigeons that had once been so numerous in the city vanished, every one, and pet dogs and cats were meeting the same fate. Now but one meal a day, and a scanty one at that, broke the fast of the besieged Kiyans. And instead of the old variety of meat and poultry and bread, of garden vegetables dried or fresh, of fish, of honey for sweet and mead and kvas for drink, they had to be satisfied with a spoonful or two of millet, lumpy for having been cooked in too little water.

For, even worse, thirst began to torment them. Some wells had days ago dried up. And others were so depleted that after drawing a bucket or two one had to wait and wait for more water to seep in. At last, within three weeks, in all the city there remained only three wells that still yielded some water. To prevent quarrels, fist fights and worse, guardsmen were posted at each of these to keep the peace.

The few cattle and horses left in the citadel also suffered, for the way to the river Libied, across the field of barrows and down the slope off the bluff, where it had been customary to drive them for their daily drink, was cut off by the horde of Pechenihs camped all along the way.

Unhappily, as if on purpose, each day that passed was rainless. In all that terrible month there were but two days of rain. And those came near the beginning, when water was still plentiful. Now people daily scanned the skies for storm. But each day they saw only the fleecy white clouds of fine weather go rolling by overhead, as if to taunt them.

The guards posted on that part of the city wall that overlooked the Dnipro gazed with afflicted eyes upon all that water flowing uselessly past, in which, moreover, swam myriad of fish to be had merely for the dipping of the net. They stared yearning at the great forest opposite, remembering the delicious little streams coursing through it and the teeming game it held—the deer, the wild boar, and the aurochs.

In such grave circumstances people's attention naturally turns to the mystery that abides unseen on earth and animates all nature. Kiyans were especially troubled that the celebration of the most solemn holy days of the entire year had been so crudely interrupted. This must be why their grandsires, the guardians of their welfare, had so far not come to their rescue.

But Kiyans were not a people who believed in destiny or doom. Therefore they tried everything they knew to bend the mysterious powers to their aid. The little jars of honey and other such small sacrifices that were placed under a certain sacred oak in the city doubled and tripled in number.

Some of the plain people even took to going to the Princess' chapel in the city, with the thought that since their own gods were withholding their luck, then perhaps this Christ in whom the Princess had placed her faith would prove more generous. Daily, the old Princess herself, ailing though she was, issued from her castle and, supported at either arm, made her way to the chapel a few steps away.

As for Bern, it was not entirely the hunger and the thirst that troubled him. They were the lesser causes of his despair.

What of it that he now had the niche behind the church? He found that it did not answer his needs after all. For, in spite of the niche, he belonged nowhere, belonged to no one. Belonged to no one. That was it. He nodded in satisfaction over having found the name of his misery.

Then his thoughts disintegrated. That happened often these days. He sat trying to gather them together again, like a herdsman with a scattered flock upon the steppe, who no sooner did he gather the sheep on this side than they escaped on that.

Now. At last. Belonged to no one.

He thought that over.

But there was remedy for that! All he needed to do—and now he marveled that he had not thought of such a simple remedy before—was to rejoin the Pechenihs. He would be accepted at last, and even though it would be on their terms, of course, at least he would have his proper and unquestioned place.

They would be only too glad. For they were a people who understood servitude—and that was more than could be said of such as the mistress. After all, wasn't he a stranger here—just as Elek had as good as said? And on top of everything, Bern reminded himself, he would get food and drink.

Of course, it was quite plain by now that the Kiyans were already beaten. In a few days hunger and thirst

—but mostly thirst—would deal them the death blow. The Pechenihs, approaching the gates, as daily they did, would reach them unopposed at last, and would force them. They would come pouring into the city. Then Bern, cap on head, would simply and quite boldly step forward and speak to them in their own tongue. And they would welcome him back with open arms.

They would plunder and ravage the city, killing the old and the weak and seizing the rest. Then, gleeful over the riches gained, they would leave the murdered city to rot in the sun and, burdened with captives and goods, make their way back to their haunts far to the south. There they would be further rewarded by the Greek emperor, if they were indeed in his pay in this invasion, as was everywhere said.

Without lifting a finger, therefore, Bern would be reunited with the Pechenihs.

But wait. Was that how it would happen?

Bern thought it over. The Pechenihs, mounted and yowling terror, would come storming into the city and cut down every living being in sight. Even if there were time for questions, no Pechenih, his blood lust heated to boiling, would ask one. Bern smiled wryly to himself. He had been a fool to think for a moment that he would be spared when the Pechenihs came.

He would have to think of some other plan.

But now he struggled to his feet. He would go search for a scrap of something to eat in the city. He stood a moment to quiet the dizziness and made sure that his cap was safe in his bosom. Only then did he set forth.

18 Not hunger, nor even thirst, but despair would break the city's will and let the Pechenih in. Already, here and there, surrender was a whispered word, but only by a few as yet. "Surrender—that's but another word for death, isn't it?" some pointed out.

And they were right in this, of course. Bern, for one, knew it.

During all this time the Princess remained in her castle in the citadel with her three young grandsons, and no word came from her to the people. There was a time, some remembered, when she would have somehow led them forth out of danger, would have defended the city with vigor and cunning. Only recall with what artfulness and how unshrinkingly she had dealt with the Derevlians. But now she was old, and ailing as well, and the predicament of her people seemed beyond her strength to overcome.

As for Sviatoslau their Prince, in vain did Kiyans await him. Though day after day the anxious guards atop the wall kept scanning the approaches to the city from the south, there was not a sign of him.

For all his valor and his enterprise, Prince Sviatoslau seemed in truth to have abandoned them. Mur-

149

murs against him grew to muttering and the muttering to audible resentment. The word was going everywhere around: "While seeking others' lands he loses his own."

At last one day, after the people had waited for some weeks, they turned to their old custom whenever some question needed debate and decision during a ruling prince's absence or because of default on his part. On their own initiative, they assembled to take counsel. In times past they had usually met in the Old Women's Market. But since that was now impossible, they gathered in the small marketplace just within the city gate.

Bern, coming upon the assembly while he was foraging for food, stood on the edge of it listening.

"But that's what I say," a man at the front of the crowd was speaking out. "Even if Pretich could cross over and come to our aid, his force is too small to rout them. Why, from what those on the wall tell us, the horde must number in the thousands!"

"That's true!" a voice called out. "And here's another thing: how are Pretich's men armed? If they've been hunting, probably all their arrows are spent."

"So then what are we to do, good people?" a woman's voice rose. "Lie down and die? I for one am not ready for that!"

A silence fell, and then a man near the front of the crowd said, "Some ruse is called for here, that's plain."

"True, and I wonder that the Princess has not thought of one. You remember how she outwitted the Derevlians that time—"

"—and with such a simple ruse!"

"The simpler the better, I always say, for then it's

less likely to go awry."

"But it's strange she has not thought of one . . ."

"Ah, but just remember, neighbor, that she's no longer young and full of the juices of life. She thinks now more of the other world than this."

"Yes, but her people?" a woman's voice spoke up. "Should she not take thought for us? If not she, then who? Tell me that! With Sviatoslau off adventuring—" she broke off angrily.

"Well, then, good people, our last and only hope is Pretich, for the drowning man must snatch even at a straw. We must send him word that we are at the end of our endurance, that our children are dying before our eyes, and that he must come at once to our relief with whatever trick he can best contrive."

"But that's the rub, neighbor," another man put in. "How to get word across?"

"Why, swim across—obviously!"

"But, my good man, do you know what you're asking? Whoever dared try it would first have to make his way down the steep bluff facing the river— and that's almost as bare as a bone, remember—and steal through the forest all the way to the river. There—"

"If," someone broke in, "he gets even that far. Someone tried reaching the river yesterday, it seems. He was caught before he even got to the bottom of the bluff and was done in on the spot."

"And then, brothers, there's the little matter of getting past the Pechenihs along the river shore. They keep a tight patrol all up and down the river, I've heard."

"True. And in any case how's anyone to swim the

river now, with the water so turbulent and swollen with the spring melt? Just answer that, if you can!"

"But is there no one among us willing to try? It's either that or surrender . . ."

Bern drifted away. Slowly, thoughtfully, he made his way home.

He sat in his niche staring into the weeds until he fell asleep. That happened often now, even in broad daylight.

During that sleep, the plan formed itself without Bern's presence, so to speak. For, the moment he woke, toward noon, he knew what he had to do.

For a long while, however, he lay half awake, watching a flock of sparrows dropping down among the dead weeds, then flying up and away over the wall. And he had the thought that a bird could cross that wall freely, while a person had to scheme to do so.

At last he got to his feet. Making sure that his cap lay in his bosom—for that cap was now crucial to his scheme—he set forth on his errand.

Once around the corner of the church, he made straight for the castle. Yet, however resolutely he walked along, all the while something in him kept shouting till his ears throbbed, "Someone stop me!"

But not a soul was astir all the way to the castle. Reaching it, Bern walked up to the door, where the guard always stood. He was quaking inside. But he got the words out. "I've come to volunteer," he said.

The guard peered down at him. "Volunteer?" he repeated, as if he hadn't understood.

"To swim the river," Bern explained.

At this, the guard looked Bern up and down with a quizzical look in his eye and, having thus taken his puny measure, snorted with feeble amusement. "Listen to it, will you?" he said. "Brave men have offered themselves—so what makes you think you'll succeed?"

"It isn't the bravery . . ." Bern murmured, stung by the remark. But for some reason the guard's disdain only strengthened his purpose.

"Not the bravery, he says!"

"I was only thinking," Bern went on, more boldly now, "that since I know the Pechenih tongue—"

The guard's eyes narrowed with sudden suspicion. "Know the Pechenih tongue?" he repeated. "And how's that?"

But before Bern could answer, he said, "Wait right here."

And he disappeared through the doorway behind him. In a few moments he reappeared and wordlessly, with a jerk of his head, summoned Bern to follow.

Before Bern knew it, he was inside the castle, in a small chamber near the entry that evidently served as a guardroom. He stood surrounded by guardsmen listening to him lay out his plan.

Bern directed his words to their commander, a young man, but with lines deep and harsh around his mouth. Not for an instant did he take his sea-blue eyes off Bern as he listened.

"I know the Pechenih tongue," Bern said, barely able to keep from giving way under that stare. "So I could get through without trouble and so reach the river and—"

The commander interrupted. "But how is it you know their tongue?" he asked.

Bern explained and then, at the commander's noncommittal nod, continued unfolding his scheme. When he was finished, he stood waiting. But already he noted that selfsame look of suspicion in the commander's eyes. In spite of himself, Bern had to glance away.

The commander stood with a frown of doubt on his long Norse face. The other guardsmen then gathered close around him and in whispers they held council, only isolated words of which Bern could hear. At last the commander said, his voice raised a little now, "That's a possible outcome, of course. Still, he might be our best chance since he knows the tongue, and I for one think we ought to risk it."

Murmurs of assent came from the others.

"But," the commander went on, "this is too chancy a matter for us to decide. Let the Princess decide— she's in command of us."

The Princess! Bern was stunned. What had he got himself into? The Princess was known for her easy anger, her shrewdness, her severity. Some even called it harshness. For all his scheming, Bern had not counted on this. He might deceive a guardsman, with luck. But the Princess?

His purpose began melting fast away. He darted his eyes from side to side. But there was no escape. Even if he ran, he was marked now, and they'd only pluck him up again.

"If there's flaw in the scheme," the commander was saying, "she'll find it out, never fear!"

So saying, with a nod and a look to the others that said, "Watch the boy," he left the room.

Bern did not move from the spot where he stood. Some of the guards now lounged against the walls, which were hung with swords and shields and bows.

154

A small group returned to their game of knucklebones in a corner.

Time passed and the commander did not return. By now Bern was rapidly losing heart, for if they did not agree to his scheme, he would surely have to suffer the common fate of the Kiyans, after all. At the same time, against all sense, he was gaining hope, for it began to look as if he would not have to face the Princess. For the moment he could not decide which was the worse.

And here at last the commander returned. "Now, then," he said to Bern, "just come along with me."

Bern followed the commander out of the room. Almost at a run, they hurried along narrow winding passages into the very depths of the castle. They made so many turnings, seemingly in every direction, that Bern felt that if he should be abandoned on the spot, he would never find his way out of the castle again. Then they began climbing up a stone staircase that went round and round and round seemingly without end. They must be climbing to the top of the stone tower.

At last, when Bern's legs were about to give out under him, they came to a low, narrow door before which stood a guardsman. At the commander's nod he stepped aside. But just as Bern made move to follow, the guardsman blocked his way. "Not you," he said. "These are the Princess' private chambers."

In the next moment, the door opened again and the commander reappeared. "Come," he said to Bern.

Obediently, Bern stepped forward and into the room.

It was a large chamber and shadowed, in spite of the daylight coming through openings in the walls to the left and the right. For a moment Bern could see nothing clearly.

He was aware that the wall straight ahead of him was covered with a great hanging of cloth that was in almost imperceptible but constant motion, as if zephyrs were wafting through the room. It was shot with shimmering threads.

But now he saw that in an enormous chair in front of the hanging someone was seated. The face, however, was shadowed. On one side of the chair stood a man, on the other a young woman in a long gown edged in fur.

The commander stepped forward, bowed deep, then said, "I have brought you the boy, Princess."

Then, stepping aside, he gave Bern a nod.

Bern stood waiting. His soul was in his heels.

 The Princess' hand, like a withered leaf, appeared from among the folds of her gown and beckoned to Bern with a single slow gesture. A broad bracelet of gold, embossed with a bold design, circled the wrist halfway to the elbow. Bern had seen such ornaments among the Pechenihs, for not infrequently they gained such treasures in booty.

The sleeve was cuffed with a rich dark brown fur. And there was fur along the edge of the gown that rested on the floor. A narrow band of the same fur held the coif on her head in place.

Obediently Bern approached. When he reached within a man's length from the Princess, he halted.

In spite of all he could do, the Princess' eyes riveted his attention for a moment. They were old eyes, large and deep set, and their source so profound that it was lost somewhere in their depths. Looking into them, Bern knew that although they might deceive, they could only with difficulty be deceived.

Perhaps once upon a time the eyes had laughed, but that was very long ago. They could no longer be surprised.

Now the Princess spoke. "Leave me," she said.

157

"Leave me with this boy." She turned her head slightly and said to the woman, "You, too, Malusha."

Her voice was low but it was vivid, belying the frailness of the hand.

The man and the woman murmured something, bowed, and retired. Bern's guard vanished.

Bern was alone with the Princess.

"Come closer, boy."

Bern stepped forward. He did not dare look up.

"Look at me!" The voice spoke with a hint of sharpness.

Slowly, with great reluctance and dread, Bern lifted his head.

"They did not tell me your name."

"Bern," he murmured.

"Bern," the voice repeated. "But I want you to speak up, Bern." There was a slight pause, during which the Princess considered him. "Now tell me, how is it you know the Pechenih tongue?"

Bern told her.

"And what was your life among them? But you must look at the person you speak to. Has no one told you that?" There was the hint of sharpness again.

With an effort Bern lifted his face. In a timid voice he began to tell some of what he remembered of his life among the nomads. When he saw with what interest she was listening, he began to tell more. He told of the steppe and of the wild horse and of galloping with the wind across the steppe. The Princess' eyes kept listening and weighing.

With less and less faltering now, he told how at night, under the dark, spangled sky, he sat on the edge of the group around the campfire with the boundless steppe at his back. He spoke of the carefree wandering.

"But you were their captive?" the Princess suddenly asked.

That brought him up short. He stopped and hung his head.

"Go on," the Princess commanded.

Something told Bern to speak no more of his life among the Pechenihs. Instead, unhindered by the Princess, he turned to his capture by Long Face, his life in the master tiler's household, and his life during the siege. Again and again he returned to the fact that his masters had turned him out on his own. But the Princess did not seem to look upon this as outrage.

Now and again she interrupted with a question. No one had ever asked him such questions before. No one had ever listened before. As he talked on, he found himself telling even of needless things, such as his visits to the church that she was having built.

As he spoke of that, for the first time the Princess' eyes smiled. "You would be a builder, then?" she remarked.

He had said not a word of that. How had she known? Better to speak no more.

He stopped and stood waiting.

The Princess allowed a deep silence. Bern glanced up at her, then quickly down, for she was gazing at him. "Now," she asked, "what is this scheme of yours that they told me of?"

The question suddenly brought Bern back to his purpose. In talking to the Princess, he had all but forgotten it. And now here was the time for greatest caution, lest he give himself away.

Choosing his words with all the care he knew, he laid it out, thus and so. Taking with him a bridle, he would be let down over the wall facing the river. He would then make his way to the Pechenih camp down there in the harbor quarter. Then—and this was the clever part—with the bridle in hand he would go through the camp asking in the Pechenih tongue whether anyone had seen a stray horse. So that, moving always toward the river, he would at length succeed in reaching it, for they would think that he was one of themselves. He would then fling off his clothes, plunge in, and swim to the other side. There—

The Princess interrupted. "The moment you began swimming, they would send arrows into you."

Bern paused. He hadn't thought of that. But no matter. He had no intention of plunging into the river, much less of swimming across. "No matter," he said.

"No matter?" the Princess repeated. "But that will take courage . . ."

Bern paused to consider that. "But," she had said. As if to say that he had no courage. He glanced at her, then hurriedly away. What had she guessed about him?

"And what," the Princess resumed, "do you propose to do on the other side?"

This time Bern took more careful thought. "I would tell them," he said, "to send force to your—that is, to our rescue."

Bern sighed. There. He had told the whole plan.

For some moments the Princess was silent, looking at him. Then, as if she had discovered something, she said, "What, exactly, prompts you to this deed?"

Bern, caught completely by surprise, let his mouth

161

drop open. No one had yet asked him this question, this all important question. He shut his mouth without uttering a word.

"For," the Princess went on when she saw that no answer was forthcoming from him, "if you fail in it, you stand to be caught and made captive again by the Pechenihs and—"

She stopped and, looking at him, her eyes widened slightly.

Bern hung his head. He had lost.

Unless—suddenly, he stuck his hand into his tunic and pulled out his cap. "This is a Pechenih cap," he explained eagerly.

He held it out to the Princess, but she did not take it.

"If I wear it while going through their camp, they'll not fail to think me one of them," Bern went on, helpless to keep the eagerness out of his voice. "See?" he said. And he put the cap on.

The Princess shut her eyes. "Put it away," she said.

In despair, Bern did as he was told.

For a long while after that the Princess sat in thought, her elbow on the arm of her chair and her chin in her hand. When at last she spoke, to Bern's surprise she did not speak of his scheme at all. Instead, as if she had already forgotten that, as well as all that had gone before, she asked a question, a most curious one. "Who made you always the stranger, Bern?"

The question was such a startling one that Bern stood at a loss for reply.

"Was it not yourself?" the Princess went on. "For, what you are to yourself you are to others. Did you know that?"

Resentment welled up in Bern's throat. It was all very well for her to say, who was clearly a princess to herself just as she was to others, who had never been on the edge of any group, but always to the fore.

"Of course," she continued, her voice as smooth as silk, "a certain courage is required . . ."

There was that word "courage" again.

"But then," she went on, "everyone is afraid at times. Only, one must not make a habit of fear."

Bern made no reply. He had lost all hope for his scheme. Obviously she had not seen any merit in it and was showing this by ignoring it.

"As for your scheme," she continued, "that is a two-faced coin. It might somehow lead to our liberation from the siege. On the other hand, it could also lead the Pechenih through our gates, if he knew of our weakness . . ."

Bern did not dare look up. How had he managed to reveal his true intent to her? Not by what he had said, surely? But perhaps this woman, old and so feeble that she might be swayed by any little breeze, had some special gift of sight. There were people like that in the world.

Bern wanted to hide.

Now for the first time the Princess leaned forward a little. "Now, Bern, listen to me," she said. "Tomorrow, when you reach the other side, take this message to commander Pretich from our people. Tell him that we are starving and thirsting. Tell him that unless he comes to our rescue without delay we must surrender to the Pechenihs."

The Princess paused a moment. "Now listen most carefully to what I am going to tell you of a scheme that may turn the trick and bring fortune to our side. It is by no means an untried one. For, simple though it is, a like ruse once deceived a foe not nearly so simple as the Pechenih."

Bern listened.

At last, the Princess finished. "We shall see what comes of this ruse," she said. "In any event, I will be ready with my grandsons." She straightened in her chair again. "Now, then, Bern, repeat all this that I have just told you."

Bern, still unable to believe his good fortune, repeated everything the Princess had said, almost word for word. When he had finished, she nodded approval. "I will rely upon you," she said.

Then, as if at some signal, the woman named Malusha reappeared. At the same moment, the guard returned to Bern's side. The Princess looked at Bern. And then she said something utterly perplexing. "Remember, Bern, it's not for others, but for you to choose. And may God bless and keep you."

A few moments later, as Bern followed the guardsman rapidly out of the castle, he could hardly keep from gloating visibly. He had deceived the Princess after all.

At the approach of dusk that same day Bern stood on the battlement atop the wall overlooking the Dnipro. With his liking for structures of all kinds, ordinarily he would have been excited over this rare and close look at the massive wall and all its parts. But, on this eve of his final departure from Kiev and Kiyans, he moved as in a dream.

He stood gazing through an opening of the battlement at what was laid out below him. Down in the harbor quarter, between the black ruins of huts and other structures along the lanes and streets, tents were pitched and half a hundred campfires burned bright. The last meal of the day was being prepared. Clouds of dust all the way to the river shore told that droves of horses were being herded down to the water for the evening's drink. The scene awakened a whole trail of memories in Bern of just such familiar twilights on the steppe, when the sun, as now, would soon begin to sink below the edge of the world. There in that camp was all the home he knew.

The younger of the two guardsmen standing beside him said, with that odd Norse lilt with which most of the guardsmen spoke, "It's good that the sun's behind us, for the wall on this side's already in shadow. So there's less danger they'll spy you out."

Bern made no reply, but watched the great river flowing grandly past. Across it, along the opposite shore, he could see a number of campfires and long dark spots that must be boats beached on the shore. Behind these loomed the dark forest stretching far beyond the limits of vision.

None of it was real. Even the sun seemed to be standing still in the sky behind them as Kiyans said it did for a single eerie instant on Midsummer's Day each year.

Unbelievable, his good luck! It was as though fortune were at last trying to make amends to him for the ills she had brought him—almost all his life, one might say. He had not been able to return to the Pechenihs on the steppe, and so here fortune had brought the Pechenihs to him! Now at last he would leave these people eternally calling themselves "we Kiyans," who looked on him with more suspicion than if he were actually a Pechenih, who denied that he was one of them—as if he had somehow to prove it—and who, worst of all, failed in their obligations as masters.

Bern looked down on the Pechenih camp again. For the first time he noticed a tent somewhat taller and larger than the others, clustered round with smaller tents. In some excitement he pointed it out to the guardsmen and said, "That's a chief's tent."

"So we have thought," the older of the guardsmen replied. He eyed Bern. "You're just a youngster," he remarked, "but it seems you have a man's courage."

Bern frowned. There was that word again.

"May luck be with you!" the younger one put in. "At least that our Princess and her grandsons be saved. For without her, we . . ." His voice trailed off.

Here at last came the commander who had accompanied Bern to his audience with the Princess. He had a bridle in his hand. "Here's what you asked for," he said, tossing it to Bern.

Bern caught it and stood dangling it from his hand. It was quite useless, of course, for he would not need it. He would simply walk up to the first Pechenih he saw and say—

"I wouldn't want to be standing in your boots!" the commander exclaimed, a note of admiration in his rough voice. He grinned. "If you're caught, they'll tear you limb from limb," he said cheerfully. He looked Bern up and down, and shook his helmeted head with ironic amusement.

Bern made no reply, for he was hearing everything as from afar.

"But come," the commander went on, his blue eyes sobering. "Time to go! Word has been sent up and down the battlement that one of ours is going over the wall, so they'll withhold their bowshots."

The two guardsmen were securing a rope ladder to the battlement. At last they stepped aside and the older gave Bern a nod. "Ready," he said.

The commander turned toward Bern and said, "Off with you. As soon as you touch bottom, give the ladder three tugs and we'll haul it back up. Good luck."

Without a single word, still clutching the bridle, Bern hoisted himself into the opening. Poised on the ledge, he dropped the end of the ladder, seized hold of the rope, and at once began the long climb to the bottom of the wall.

Softly the guards called after him. "Take care, brother!"

And, "Good luck, brother . . ."

Bern climbed down as rapidly as he could. This was the most dangerous part of his venture, for if the Pechenihs caught sight of him now, taking him for a Kiyan—not knowing that he was actually one with them—they would send an arrow into him. They were excellent shots and could shoot even a speeding hare at three hundred paces.

At last Bern's feet touched ground. He gave the ladder three tugs and at once it began jerking rapidly upward. He stood watching it for an instant, a feeling of bitter finality growing in him. He was quit of Kiev and Kiyans forever.

Along this part of the wall, fortunately or unfortunately—it was hard to decide which—there was no ditch along the bottom. Instead, the ground fell away from the wall in a steep slope. As Bern began making his way down it he found it as treacherous as ice underfoot, for the ground here was bare and gravelly.

Several times his feet slid out from under him and he sat down suddenly. Each time, he looked swiftly about to make sure he had not alerted some Pechenih. He knew he was being watched from above.

At last, in a small avalanche of gravel, he reached the edge of the swamp forest. Scrambling to his feet, he made a lunge for the trees.

Panting heavily, he dropped to the ground to rest for a moment. Here he was safe—for the time. While catching his breath, he gazed about. The forest was wrapped in deep dusk. A few late birds still flitted about but there hung a kind of pause on the air, like that on the steppe at dusk when the day creatures are bedding down for the night and the night creatures are bestirring themselves for the hunt. How peaceful it was . . .

But the forest was no friend of his. It was as hostile, as treacherous as people. Fumbling in his tunic, he drew out his cap and put it on. In the event he met with a Pechenih in the forest the cap might prevent his being killed on the spot. Now he started on again, leaping from hummock to hummock, moving toward his right, where lay the harbor quarter.

Somewhere to his left, on the bank of the little stream deep within the forest, had burned the balefire he had attended. Now, of course, nothing remained of that brave welcome to the returning spirits of old Kiyans. It was a charred ruin, dead.

Bern halted, surprised by the pang of regret he felt at this thought, as if the balefire signified some happy and even momentous event in his life. He remembered the oneness he had felt with that fire, and even with those sitting around it. In the next moment he was struggling against a bitter and terrible grief over what he was doing.

But—there was no one to restrain him from the deed.

He hurried on. The forest was beginning to thin and in another few moments he reached the edge of it. Crouching behind a shrub, he peered out at the camp pitched in the harbor quarter.

He was shocked by the change. Gone was the bustle surrounding the harbor, with its ships and its seamen. The huts that had lined the lanes were heaps of cinders, every one. The wattle fences had been knocked down and trampled in the dust. Bern tried to find the hut of Long Face. Impossible. Not a hut, not a fence remained.

Everywhere he looked now, as far as he could see, were tents. He shut his eyes and gave his head a shake so as somehow to sort his thoughts. When he opened them again, the scene had already begun to be familiar again, and he was consoled by this.

The men were at their twilight tasks, building up the fires, stirring pots, carrying buckets of water up from the river. Others were moving about among the drove of horses to the right. Nearby, a group of youths circled a pair engaged in a wrestling match.

Eagerly Bern searched among the faces for a familiar one. But he saw none. With hungry fascination he stared at a hound lapping at a bowlful of something held by a youth who was sharing his food with the animal.

But while Bern crouched there, a breeze from the direction of the camp brought him an almost overpowering stench of manure, of sour milk and dust all intermingled.

At once, with but that single whiff it was all brought back to Bern, all those things that he had forgotten.

He had forgotten the endless treks, hot and dusty, across the parched, denuded land, the long fasts when hunger gnawed him while the masters ate, the thirst, the flies and lice and tormenting gnats, the howling winds of winter.

He had forgotten the monotony and the very uselessness of the existence of the nomad, who built nothing more permanent or noble than a flimsy sheep pen upon the steppe and who destroyed, besides, all that he touched that others had built.

Over and over, as he gazed at the scene in front of him, he was struck with what he had forgotten. But what astounded him most of all was that he had completely forgotten the very fact of his captivity.

True, while he had been the Pechenihs' captive they had never troubled to fetter him or lock him up. But even so, where would he have run to? As far as one could see in every direction was but sky and grass and wind. A lone person in that immensity would have soon found himself helpless, held firm in space so vast that one could not see the walls of it.

Yet, for all its immensity, the steppe had been his prison. In all his extravagant remembrances of the steppe, not until now did he know that this was so.

He glanced behind him. No, he could not go back.

"What have I done? What have I done?" he whispered aloud.

Even if he succeeded in reaching the wall again, or even the city gate—he had locked himself out of that world forever.

He did not know how long he crouched there, dreading to go forth and unable to turn back, when to his alarm, the hound suddenly came trotting toward the bush behind which he was hiding. Halting in front of it, it pricked up its ears and pointed. Then it growled low in its throat.

At this, several heads in the camp looked in its direction, then turned away.

Continuing to point, the dog began baying at Bern. At this, several of the men half rose and stared into the forest.

If Bern stayed where he was, he would be discovered. And then and there, that would be the end of him.

He made a decision. To save himself at all he would have to come out. He would make straight for the chief's tent. There he would go up to the chief and say, "I've come back."

To buy his life, he would undoubtedly have to tell what he knew of the situation in the city.

He stood, took a deep breath, and came dashing out from behind the shrub. A few more faces turned toward him, puzzled; a few more figures rose to their feet.

Swinging and jingling the bridle as he came running into the camp, Bern shouted, "Who's seen my horse? Who's seen my grey?"

The cap on his head was the saving of him, for noting it, the figures sat down again. Straight ahead now Bern caught sight of the chief's tent and made for it. As he came running up, he saw the chief himself squatting beside the campfire, surrounded by his men.

"I've come—I've come . . ." Bern had to stop for breath.

As he stood there panting, the Pechenihs, their curiosity aroused, got to their feet and stood eyeing him with growing suspicion. Bern looked from face to face. They were familiar enough, every one.

But suddenly they were utterly alien to him.

"It's not for others but for you to choose."

Those words of the Princess Olha suddenly came into his head. He had chosen. But he had chosen wrong, for he had walked straight into the camp of his enemy. The stench that filled his nostrils told him so. The sullen faces told him so.

172

And who among the Pechenihs had ever called him brother?

Whether Kiyans liked it or not, he chose to be one of them. That being so—

Behind him was the river. With a sudden movement he snatched the cap off his head, flung both cap and bridle into the faces of his enemy, then wheeled and ran. A howl of anger broke out behind him.

Straight for the river he raced. Behind him the pounding of feet and the wild yells grew louder, closer. Veering like the hare to escape, Bern tore through the camp.

At last—the dock. He dashed to the very end of it and plunged in. Frantically his arms and legs churned him away from shore. In the next instant something sang past his ears and a rain of singing arrows splashed all around him.

Bern ducked his head, kicked his feet, and plunged under. Several times he had to surface for air. When he reached the current, out of bowshot at last, he surfaced for good.

Before striking out for the opposite shore, he turned over on his back for an instant and looked up at the darkening sky. Suddenly he smiled.

And for the first time in his life the smile was a smile of triumph.

The people remembered. More than a century later, long after these events in the life of the city of Kiev, the first chronicler of the land wrote as follows.

In the year 968, the Pechenihs came for the first time. But Sviatoslau was absent. Olha shut herself up in the citadel of Kiev with her grandsons: The Pechenihs besieged the citadel with a great force, with a countless multitude all around the citadel, and it was impossible to steal out of the city or to send news.

The people were at last weakened by famine and thirst. Those who had taken to the other side of the Dnipro in boats stayed on that side and it was impossible for even a single one to enter Kiev or to go out of the city to them. On account of the Pechenihs, it was impossible to water the horses in the Libied. The people in the city, tormented to extremity, said, "Is there someone who might be able to get to the other side and tell them that if they do not steal up to the city by morning, we must give ourselves up to the Pechenihs?"

One boy said, "I will do it."

And they said, "Go."

He then went out of the city with a bridle and ran

throughout the Pechenih camp, saying, "Has anyone seen my horse?"

Because he knew the Pechenih tongue, they took him for their own. When he reached the river, he threw off his trousers, dove into the Dnipro, and began to cross over.

When the Pechenihs saw him, they chased headlong after him, shooting at him. But by then they could do nothing.

Then the people on the other side saw him and paddled out in a boat to meet him. They took him into the boat and brought him to the princely guard. He said to them, "If you do not steal up to the city on the morrow, the people are ready to give themselves up to the Pechenihs."

Then their commander, Pretich by name, said, "We will steal up in boats tomorrow morning and take the Princess and the princes by force and carry them away to this side. If we don't succeed in doing this, Sviatoslau will seize and destroy us."

On the morrow, toward daybreak, they embarked in boats and blew loud blasts on their trumpets and the people within the city raised a shout.

The Pechenihs, thinking that the Prince was approaching, fled from the city in different directions. And Olha descended to the boats with her grandsons and her retinue.

Seeing this, the prince of the Pechenihs returned alone to commander Pretich and said, "Who was it that came?"

Pretich said to him, "People from the other side."

The prince of the Pechenihs said, "And are you the Prince?"

But Pretich said, "I am his man and I am come with

his vanguard. And after me comes the Prince with his regiments, countless multitudes."

That's what he said, to threaten the Pechenihs.

. . . And the Pechenihs withdrew from the city . . .

The Kiyans sent word to Sviatoslau, saying, "You, Prince, rove about seeking foreign lands, but your own you have abandoned. The Pechenihs all but seized us and your mother and your children. Now if you don't come and defend us, they will indeed seize us. Are you not at all sorry for your native land, your mother, who is old, and your children?"

Hearing this, Sviatoslau at once mounted his horse and with his guard came to Kiev. He kissed his mother and his children, and lamented the hurt they had suffered at the hands of the Pechenihs. He gathered warriors and drove the Pechenihs away into the steppe. And there was peace.

As for the boy who had swum the river and risked his life to save his city and his people, there seemed no need to mention his name. For even then, a century and more later, all knew it: Bern the master builder, son of Mikula.